MW00423750

OUTLAW TRAVELER

AMAZON HEAT

DENNIS HAMBRIGHT

Outlaw Traveler - Amazon Heat

Copyright © 2021 by Dennis Hambright

ISBN (Print): 978-1-09838-309-1
ISBN (eBook): 978-1-09838-310-7

Author's Website: DennisHambright.com
Cover Design: www.DerangedDoctorDesign.com

What matters most is how well you walk through the fire.
— Charles Bukowski

Nobody's bleeding. Nobody's dead. It's a good day.
— Damien Chance

PROLOGUE

T HE weather was typical for December in the Amazon basin. It rained throughout the night, and now in these first hours of morning the sun drew up a heavy mist to hang as a shroud above the dense tropical growth. It was a picture-postcard view, like something you'd expect to see on the cover of *National Geographic*. Deep valleys slashed through the mountains with the power of nature and the patience of thousands of years. Surely no man could look upon the vast emerald blanket of tropical growth, feel the unremitting power from the constant roar of the river humming though his body, and not believe that some higher hand had carved it all out with divine inspiration.

I was perched high on the side of a steep ridge, secluded beneath a thick stand of banana trees, watching the morning unfold in the valley below. I'd carefully chosen this position, so I'd have an unobstructed view of the half-moon shaped clearing cut into the jungle along the far side of the river.

There were four recently constructed buildings that scarred the otherwise pristine landscape. Primitive, with plywood walls and corrugated tin roofs, they were a far cry from the bamboo and thatch huts the local *campesinos* would be able to afford to build for themselves. There were two long, low-slung narrow structures to be used as warehouses, one building with a satellite dish cantilevered off the roof at an awkward angle to serve as an office and communications shack, and a fourth structure for living quarters. The intel I'd gotten indicated there would be a maximum of eight men housed there to guard the facility until it was ready for full operation.

I'd painstakingly situated myself in position four days ago. It was an arduous day and a half journey of slashing my way through the dense growth over the backside of the mountain. Prior to that, a two-day trip traveling up-river stuffed in a thirty-foot dugout canoe with a half dozen local natives. I'd prospected for gold in the area before and they knew if I found a promising location it might mean good paying work in my camp. As always, they went out of their way to wish me luck.

I already had over seven days of hard bush time just getting to this point. My muscles cramped from the last few days of lying in position, and even though periods of intense isometric exercise helped, I'm not a man who enjoys inactivity. I'd been in the same old tiger-striped camouflage clothing for a week. It had been rained soaked, sweat soaked, and caked with dirt. The musty, living odor of wet ground and decaying plants clung to my skin, and with every breath the scent was thick in my nostrils and heavy in my mouth and throat. I had every reason to be on edge, but as I'd trained my mind to do, I blocked out the physical discomforts and stayed focused on the job at hand.

A quick glance at my watch and I could see that I'd been up and in position for over four hours. It was just past eight in the morning, but immersed in the depths of the jungle it's almost impossible to maintain any normal concept of time. Daylight or the pitch black of night are all that matters, and the farther you move under the triple canopy of deep bush, sometimes even those are hard to distinguish one from the other.

Stretched out on a thin mattress of palm fronds I peered out over the earthen lip of my hasty firing position. Little more than a twenty-inch-deep coffin-shaped indentation that I'd scratched out in the soft jungle floor, it would be home for as long as it took to get the job done.

I thought back to when I first started working in the jungles of South America. I'd come to prospect for gold and hunt lost treasure, and knew from the very beginning that I was born for it. Since then, I've developed an unusual knack for the life and an uncanny sixth sense that's kept me sane and alive in the harsh and unforgiving environment. Now, that intuition was kicking in. Rivulets of sweat trickled down between my shoulders, heightening the chill that ran up my spine, and I knew the twitching in my muscles was a sign that the time was near.

Within moments a distant rumble began thundering its way up the valley, validating my premonition. I raised my spotting scope and scanned the horizon, watching the shadowy form of a helicopter as it became more recognizable with each passing second, slithering its way up through the rugged contours of the valley at a dangerously low altitude in order to avoid radar detection. Looking back down to the buildings below I could see that the daring pilot must have radioed ahead to announce their impending arrival. Men clambered out of the bunkhouse and began setting up a perimeter of security.

There were five men in the clearing. Three brandished AK-47s, with their characteristic banana-shaped clips curling out below the nasty world-wide favorites for spitting out rapid-fire death and destruction. The other two cradled "street sweepers" — Auto Assault 12-gauge shotguns with bulky twenty-round drum magazines and a 300-round-per-minute firing rate — deadly for close range bush penetration.

The makeshift detail fanned out to form a ragged line of protection at the edge of the river. One man tossed a grenade that spewed a dull yellow cloud of smoke to mark the landing area while the others scanned the surrounding jungle for intruders. None of them could see more than five feet into the dense growth that surrounded their camp, so I knew the momentary show of security was nothing more than a weak attempt to stroke the enormous egos of the incoming visitors. If they had any real concerns for security, they would have had foot patrols and dogs out scouring the bush for perpetrators.

As the sentries took their final positions, the Bell Ranger streaked out over the tight cluster of buildings and across the river into a wildly exaggerated aerial power slide, pushing high up the ridge above me. More useless theatrics. Well camouflaged and concealed beneath the broad hands of the banana palms, I wasn't concerned about my location being compromised.

The multi-million-dollar craft swung around into an aerial pirouette and I thought about the misery and destruction of innocent life that paid for that extravagant piece of machinery. I also remembered the tragedy that its owner spat into my own life, and then focused back on the task at hand.

I reached over and pulled back the dark green poncho covering my tools, revealing a matte black Barrett 95M rifle. The .50 caliber rounds have an effective range of up to 1,800 meters and pack enough power to punch through a steel plate. I was less than 300 meters from my target with an overload of power and reach, and confident that from this distance I'd have no trouble laying the rounds one on top of the other in a tight and deadly strike pattern.

I lifted the rifle up off the poncho, and with my right hand palmed the magazine into the receiver. A sharp click let me know it was seated in place. I pulled back the bolt and fed a round into the chamber. I could feel my pulse quicken and took several slow breaths to control the anxiety of the moment. I'd fired countless rounds on the range preparing for this assignment, hitting targets under every conceivable condition. Driving rain. High crosswinds. Targets moving at different speeds and into varying positions. I knew how to adapt for every possible variable and still hit my mark. But those were steel practice targets. This would be my first time pulling the trigger on a living, breathing, flesh and bone subject. No matter how physically and mentally prepared I believed I was to do the job, the real proof lie in the moments ahead.

I pulled in one more calming breath and swallowed back the bitter taste of bile that crept up into my throat, making final preparations to move beyond my challenge of conscious. I shifted slightly and nestled into my final firing position, watching as the helicopter settled onto the rocky shoreline. The rotors whipped through the air, scattering the smoke and haze into an eerie yellow apparition, whirling up into the sky.

Belly flat to the damp ground. Back and shoulders arched upward. The butt of the rifle pulled snug to my shoulder. Right index finger resting safely outside the trigger guard. One eye peering through the scope. I'd rehearsed those same movements every day since arriving at the little encampment, just as I'd played them out in my dreams, night after tortuous night since this nightmare began.

There's a confident comfort in the familiarity, and I knew it was all more than perfectly milled and machined parts assembled into a rifle. Now, it was a unique marriage of man and metal acting as one to accomplish the task at hand. For the first time since this ordeal began, I realized that I *was* the weapon.

Only a few moments remained, the seconds dragging through molasses. The chopper rotors slowed, and the dust and debris began to settle. A sixth man emerged from the communications shack, moving quickly toward the aircraft and sliding back the rear passenger door. Every man snapped to military attention.

Stepping first from the luxury craft was an unusually large man by Latin American standards. Standing well over six feet tall, he towered over the others in a full-dress military uniform with brightly colored ribbons and medals draped ceremoniously across his chest. Through the scope I recognized him as Colonel Juan Zoto, one of Bolivia's most decorated and ruthless military leaders.

Colonel Zoto was famous for seizing every opportunity to ally himself with his country's strongest anti-North American allies, and continually rallied alongside them in their constant rhetoric and criticisms against the United States' involvement in the region. When the cameras were rolling and the U.S. was the target, he was always right there in the front row, reveling in the limelight and solidifying his position with the radical movement. I framed his face within the crosshairs and considered the depth of his hypocrisy and self-righteousness. I knew the man for the heartless thug that he really was — nothing more than an opportunist who didn't give a damn about his country or his countrymen. All he cared about was lining his own deep pockets, and if innocent blood had to be spilled for his benefit, so be it. I gently caressed the trigger. *Not this time. As much as you surely deserve it, not this time.*

Colonel Zoto moved forward, and I could see the physical tension take hold of the men as the next visitor stepped from the chopper. This newest arrival was the owner of the helicopter and the small outpost below. He also laid claim to magnificent villas scattered around the globe, a fleet of private jets and yachts, and bank accounts that rivaled the gross national product of several small nations. Most notably, he was South America's most public and flamboyant drug kingpin.

Ramiro Dueñas was on the top ten hit list of every major law enforcement agency in the world, and even though his growing list of heinous crimes was well documented, nobody had been able to bring him to justice. He traveled the world to places where cash trumped extradition, and openly boasted of his criminal enterprise while spreading wealth to dirt poor communities who regarded him as a modern-day Robin Hood. He was also a master at the age-old art of *soborno* — the South American tradition of bribery. When that didn't work, he utilized unbridled violence and terrorism to get his way.

Even in the oppressive heat and humidity of this remote jungle location, Dueñas was dressed to impress, wearing a cream-colored, custom tailored Italian suit, layered over a lavender silk shirt buttoned to the throat. Tan leather seam-stitched Prada loafers wrapped his feet. No socks. Of course, a man of his stature had to always maintain appearances. I could see the sparkle from the gaudy diamond and emerald encrusted ring on his left hand as he swept his outstretched arm about the installation, explaining to Colonel Zoto how he expected things to work.

The crude little facility was less than one kilometer from the Peruvian border and in an area once heavily patrolled by the UMOPAR (*Unidad Móvil Policial para Áreas Rurales*) — the Bolivian military's special anti-narcotics force. A fierce adversary of *los narcos*, the UMOPAR was initially trained and subsidized by the U.S. military and much more difficult to bribe than their counterparts in the regular army and local police. Often referred to as *Los Leopardos*, they were proficient and dedicated jungle warriors.

Fortunately for Dueñas, some of the military's other commanding officers were little more than high-ranking desk jockeys cut from a more economically ambitious and much less moral cloth.

Coupled with Colonel Zoto's considerable influence, the UMOPAR had their primary efforts directed halfway across the country to the Chapare Region, where the bulk of Bolivia's cocaine was produced — or so it was believed. It had cost Dueñas millions of dollars in *soborno* payments to the colonel and his associates, but he would easily make back many times that amount once operations were in full swing.

The logistics were more difficult, and it would take a much greater investment to keep things going in such a remote location, but money saved from less interference from the military and the meddling North Americans would net a much greater profit in the long run. Dueñas was especially encouraged because he'd found a new partner who'd committed to purchase almost eighty percent of what he projected he could produce here. The eager man had even given him a ten-million-dollar cash deposit to secure his first shipment. He also knew the generous percentage he'd pay Colonel Zoto would finance his political ambitions, and that would even further solidify the future of his illegal endeavors. The mountains of riches he'd amassed in the past would be a mere pittance compared to what he was on the verge of making now.

• • •

There are two primary methods for taking a target — trapping and tracking.

To trap a target, you fix your sights on a chosen point and wait for it to come to you. Pick your field of fire and be patient. When the target moves into the zone, you take the shot.

To track a target, you first acquire it within your sights, and then follow it, taking the shot when you're ready. Tracking is much more active and certain.

I peered through the scope, securing Dueñas in my sights, and then tracked him across the compound. When he stopped at the entrance to the communications shack, I adjusted my optics to bear dead center on his chest. Mass shot first.

I drew in a slow, deep breath, feeling my body go coma-calm, and stroked off the first round. A 2,710-foot-per-second hot iron fist pounded through his chest, slamming his body against the wall and crumpling him to his knees. I smoothly racked the next shell into the chamber, adjusted my sights to center just above his chin, and delivered the second round. In that instant the head of Ramiro Dueñas erupted into a violent crimson mist, spraying sticky particles of blood, brain, and skull all over those standing near him. Colonel Zoto dove for cover through the open door of the communications shack while the security detail fired randomly into the surrounding bush. Shotguns pumped round after deafening round and the AK-47s rattled off until their clips were empty.

My position was secure. The deceptive acoustics of the valley echoed the report of my rifle so there was no way for them to determine where the shots had come from. I adjusted my field of fire and placed several rounds into the tail rotor of the chopper, transforming it into a twisted mangle of useless metal and preventing them from mounting an air search for their attacker. There's no cell coverage out here in the jungle, and I knew they wouldn't use a satellite phone or the camp radio to call for assistance, and risk giving away the position of their clandestine installation to any eavesdropping authorities.

I glanced once more at the scene of mass confusion below, and then gathered up my gear, slipping farther back into the protective cover of even thicker jungle.

The headless body of Ramiro Dueñas lie in a pile of lifeless mass.

Men scrambled about aimlessly, not knowing where to return fire.

Colonel Zoto screamed incoherent orders from the safety of the communications shack.

And I knew that my life would be changed forever.

CHAPTER 1

THE tension in the room was palpable. It was the kind of atmosphere that made your throat so tight that every swallow had to be forced, and even though the office was spacious, a glove of claustrophobia squeezed uncomfortably around three of the four men present. The fourth man was at ease. This was his domain. His territory. He'd summoned the others to this impromptu gathering, and even though his outward demeanor appeared calm, everyone knew it was little more than a well-rehearsed decorative shell that belied his true self — cold, arrogant, ruthless.

J. Edward Adams III raised himself slowly from the high-back leather chair, his palms pressing deep into the soft padding of the armrests. He strained to hoist his considerable weight to a standing position, and then with an unexpected bolt of furious energy snatched an ornately carved antique walking stick and slammed it flat against the polished surface of the desk. The sharp crack echoed throughout the room, startling the other men present. Then, he carefully considered each of the three subordinates gathered for his inquisition. He stared into the eyes of the first man for several long seconds, then the next, and the next, prolonging the agonizing suspense. Finally, he focused his intense glare on the man seated to his far left across the broad expanse of dark mahogany.

"Mr. Breckenridge, I am a man of little patience for excuses, and you have been paid extremely well so I should not have to suffer an inconvenience such as this."

Realizing that he was the chosen target, Alan Breckenridge imagined that he could actually hear the shackles of anguish rattle to the floor around the other men who'd been given reprieve. He felt the grip of anxiety squeeze even tighter around his throat.

"Now, will you please enlighten me as to what you plan to do to correct this unfortunate situation?" J. Edward dumped the scalding water of responsibility right into Breckenridge's lap.

"Mr. Adams, sir, we don't know for certain what happened down south." He paused briefly, hacking a dry cough to try and knock some confidence back into his voice. "The message we received simply said that the shipment would be delayed indefinitely due to a serious breach in security, and that more detailed information would be forthcoming."

J. Edward let the words dangle precariously in the air for a moment, allowing the silence and anticipation of his reaction to cause a beaded line of sweat to crawl across the forehead of his victim. The only sound in the room was the incessant hum of fluorescent lights. "In that case, might I suggest that you be on the next available flight to Bolivia so you can be the recipient of that more detailed information?"

Breckenridge had worked for J. Edward Adams III long enough to know that it wasn't a question he was being given the opportunity to consider. It was a mandate.

"You can catch a flight that leaves in about three hours and still make all the connections tonight," said the man seated next to him. Everyone summoned to the meeting had a sneaking suspicion what it was going to be about and came as prepared as possible.

Breckenridge shot him what would have been an icy go-to-hell look, but the little weasel was too busy staring down at the tassels on his shoes to appreciate the full effect.

11

"I just thought…I was only trying to…," he stammered, realizing he had paddled into some very unwelcome waters.

"Blow me," Breckenridge suggested under his breath.

J. Edward ignored the interruption, staying focused on his chosen victim.

"Yes sir, Mr. Adams. I'll leave right away." Breckenridge gathered up his briefcase and what little pride he had left and made his way out of the office. It wasn't more than twenty feet to the door, but he felt like he was crossing the Sahara Desert, feeling the intense heat of J. Edward's stare burning into his back every step of the way.

J. Edward Adams III was indeed a man of little patience, and it was common knowledge among his associates that his wrath was violent and far-reaching for those that displeased him. And even though he strove to maintain an outward air of dignity in all matters, those he hired to do his bidding were men with less appreciation for the gentler qualities in life.

Prestigious boarding schools. Ivy League education. World travel and mingling with the upper crust of society. He lived the blue-blood life. But now, this banishment, and to *Okla-fucking-homa* of all places. "The friendly frontier, indeed," he mumbled. It was almost more than he could stand.

J. Edward shifted his bulk, trying to transfer more weight onto his walking stick and off his right leg. Even after all these years the pain was still almost unbearable. He slipped two fingers inside his shirt and rubbed the mangled old bullet he wore around his neck. Feeling the rough lead between his fingers bolstered his determination and briefly took his mind off the pain. He peered through the floor-to-ceiling windows that made up the back wall of his office. Looking out toward the evening horizon, broad strokes of purple, pink, and orange painted a glorious sunset across the Oklahoma sky. Then, he diverted his attention to the after-work traffic, stacking up bumper-to-bumper on the expressway twenty-eight stories below. He thought how appropriate it all seemed, and how beneath him they all really were — literally and figuratively. A gentle rap on his office door disrupted his thoughts, but he continued staring out into the distance, keeping his back to the intruder.

"Excuse me, sir, but I wanted to remind you about your dinner with the senator this evening. The car will be here for you at six-thirty." There were several long moments of unanswered silence, so she continued. "Will there be anything else before I leave for the day?"

"No, Mrs. Carter. Nothing." Curt with her, as always.

"Very well, sir. Good evening." She left quietly, pulling the heavy doors closed behind her.

Adele Carter had worked as J. Edward's personal assistant for six years, and he still treated her like he did her first day on the job — like she was something objectionable he'd stepped in and couldn't get scraped off the bottom of his expensive shoes.

Senator, he thought, dismissively. *Big deal.* J. Edward shook his head, repulsed at the thought of his scheduled company for the evening. *Nothing but a state senator. Why should I even waste my time?*

Fifty-seven-years old and regarded as one of the most powerful businessmen in this part of the country, he appeared to have it all — money, prestige, social standing. But like many of those rare individuals who pass over that mysterious line from mere wealth into riches that are inconceivable to most, money no longer provided the motivation he needed. He already had more money than he could spend in a dozen lifetimes. Power. That's what it was all about now, and not just common run-of-the-mill dominance that most rich men had. Hell, he had that already. He wanted "Fuck You Power", and he wanted it with a capital "F" and a capital "Y". He longed for the kind of unbridled dominance that made politicians sweat and could change the economic course of small countries — power that would make him untouchable.

J. Edward knew he had already advanced as far as he ever would within his family's organization. He also knew it was only because of the respect the others held for his father that they'd allowed him to come this far. They believed in tradition, loyalty, omertà, and all that other nonsense his old man was always preaching. But when his father died, J. Edward was sent to oversee their interests here. They thought it would keep him out of their way and under control, and that he'd be content playing the role and spending the money they allowed him. But they were wrong. He wasn't pleased with his station in life and had plans for changes — drastic changes. He was more determined than ever to show them what real power was all about, and that he didn't need the family organization or the doddering old fools that controlled it.

But now, this disruption in South America threatened to slow his progress. Those shipments and the tremendous influx of capital they would generate were essential to his plans. This wasn't acceptable. Not acceptable at all.

"Well, Breckenridge is on his way to solve the problem," he said. "He'll solve it, or I'll damn well eliminate him right along with it!" He stood alone in his office, still staring out into the distance, talking to his own reflection in the glass. These days he believed the most intelligent and productive conversations he had were the ones he had with himself.

Considering it a criminal offense to water down good liquor with ice, he swirled three fingers of straight scotch in a short crystal tumbler. He took a sip and savored the liquid warmth as it poured through him, nodding slowly, convincing himself that everything would work out just as he'd planned.

CHAPTER 2

ALAN Breckenridge thumbed the garage door remote clipped to the drive's side visor of his Audi R8 Spyder as he backed down the driveway. He stopped and watched the heavy hinged sections of the metal door rattle across the tracks, banging securely against the pavement. Then, he slammed the selector into first, spun the wheel, popped the clutch, and jammed his foot hard on the accelerator. It was all a perfectly coordinated adrenaline booster that sent the powerful car fishtailing down the alley, and off toward Will Rogers World Airport on another wild goose chase for the almighty J. Edward Adams III.

"One of these days that arrogant bastard is going to push me too far!" The stereo was cranked up so loud that the speakers vibrated with the heavy bass rhythm and he had to yell to be heard over the music. He was venting his frustration and driving erratically, whipping the sleek black German sports car in and around traffic, shifting through the six-speed manual transmission and pushing the V-10 beast for all she had. All the other drivers on I-40 were moving much too slowly for his taste. He hammered off angry bursts from his horn, swerving to change lanes and barely missing the car in front of him. He glanced down at the speedometer, slowed to eighty, downshifted to sixty, and then fell in behind an eighteen-wheeler.

"Sweetheart, please try and clam down. If you hate it so much, why don't you just quit?" Lisa Dalton, Breckenridge's fiancée, was riding with him to the airport. She leaned over and turned the radio volume down to a tolerable level. "With your background and all of your contacts, you could work anywhere you want." She grabbed the hand he'd been pounding on the center console, giving it a gentle squeeze to reassure him. "I believe in you, Alan."

At her touch, Breckenridge felt his anger and frustration begin to die down. He lightened up on the accelerator even more, sliding smoothly off onto the exit ramp for the airport.

"Thanks, baby, but it's really not that bad," he said, trying to soften the mood. "I'm just tired and pissed-off about having to make this sudden trip back down to Bolivia." He pulled his hand away, turning it over and entwining his fingers with hers, palm-to-palm. Now, he was the one squeezing to reassure her.

Breckenridge knew he could never quit, and he also knew he could never tell Lisa why. He loved her too much and was convinced that if she knew the truth about why J. Edward had such an unbreakable hold on him, he'd lose her for sure. He'd already been forced to give up too much in life as it was, and losing her would be more than he could handle.

Lisa leaned over the center console and snuggled her head into the crook between his neck and shoulder, brushing her cheek under his chin.

As they pulled up to the passenger unloading zone in front of the main terminal, Breckenridge took in their surroundings. It might be called Will Rogers World Airport, but with only one three-level terminal and never the hustle and bustle he was used to in other hubs around the globe, there wasn't anything worldly about it as far as he was concerned.

Breckenridge gently tilted Lisa's chin up with the tips of his fingers so he could look into her eyes. She had the most beautiful eyes he'd ever seen — emerald green with flecks of hazel that glittered like gold, and they'd mesmerized him from the very first time he'd seen them.

She pulled away and nestled her chin even deeper into that spot between his neck and shoulder, not wanting him to leave.

"Lisa, I've got to go, or I'll miss my flight," he whispered.

She slid back over into the passenger seat, pouted out her lower lip and hugged both knees up to her chest. The heels of her feet balanced on the front edge of the leather seat. She looked like a spoiled little girl wanting what she'd been told she couldn't have.

"Jesus, Lisa, don't look at me like that," Breckenridge moaned. "You know I don't want to go as it is. That somebody-ran-over-my-kitty look sure as hell isn't going to make it any easier."

"I know," she giggled. "I just wanted to make sure that you missed me even more." She pouted her lip out even further.

"Absolute perfection," he said, slightly under his breath. He looked again into those enchanting eyes, and then to the fullness of her lips, all of it framed by wild locks of thick blonde curls that fell well past her shoulders.

"What did you say?" She loved it when he let his tough-guy image down and said sweet little things like that.

"Nothing. I've got to go." He leaned over and gave her a quick peck on the cheek, knowing that anything more would only make leaving that much tougher. "There's no need for you to come in," he said, stepping out of the car. "I'll call you when I change planes in Dallas, and then again before I leave Miami."

When Breckenridge rose from getting his luggage out of the trunk, one heavy bag in each hand, Lisa was standing right in front of him. She was so close that he could smell a hint of cinnamon gum on her breath.

"Trapped!" she laughed, and threw both of her arms around his neck, pressing her body fully against him. "Love ya', babe," she whispered into his ear, just before spearing it with the tip of her tongue.

Breckenridge shuddered with pleasure. "What am I going to do with you?" he laughed.

"Keep me if you're smart — and if you're lucky!" she giggled.

Lisa sashayed around the car toward the open driver's door, exaggerating the swing of her hips for maximum effect. She was wearing a light pink sundress with turquoise piping around the neck and hemline. The colors perfectly complemented her tanned skin, and the silky material hung on her toned body in a way that accentuated all the right curves. She tossed her hair over her shoulder and looked back at him. Then, she smiled and slid into the car.

Breckenridge walked up the short ramp to the terminal entrance. He could hear the hi-pitched chirp of tires gripping pavement as she popped the clutch and sped away. He didn't look back. He wished he had the strength to tell her the truth.

CHAPTER 3

I LAID flat on my back, nothing between me and the uncomfortable mattress but a paper-thin sheet that did little more than serve as a rough canvas for the silhouette of sweat outlining my body. I took one more drag off an unfiltered Astoria cigarette and blew out a stream of pungent smoke, watching as the old wooden ceiling fan paddled through the humid air, scattering it around the room. Rising up on one elbow, I flicked the smoldering butt toward an open window. A fiery shower of sparks danced off the sill as it bounced out of the second story room.

Chulumani is where I feel most at home these days. It's a small town in the Sud Yungas region of Bolivia, about one-hundred-and-twenty-five kilometers from the capital city of La Paz, at the end of a treacherous stretch of the infamous *Camino de la Muerte* — The Road of Death. Nestled in the mountains and off the beaten path, the people are friendly, but keep their ranks closed tight. I've spent enough time here over the last few years that they seem to accept me as more than just another tourist — at least as much as they'll ever accept any foreigner.

There's never a word spoken about the tragedy that happened here in the past, but there are times when I still see it in their eyes, and spoken of or not, I know it hasn't been forgotten.

I reached over and clicked off the only lamp in the room, my hand brushing across the cool metal surface of the Beretta 9mm pistol lying on the bedside table.

I was sweating from the heat, but a cold chill knifed through me, just like it always did when I thought about how much my life has changed.

Life is real here. There are challenges that come about daily where a man must survive by his wits and abilities, or he dies. It's as simple as that. It truly is an adventurous existence in one of the world's last remaining frontiers. That's what I came to find, and not only did I find it, but it's changed everything that my life is about.

I closed my eyes and let my thoughts drift back to when I first came to South America. All the adventure. All the love. And now, the unbearable heartache that haunts my every dream.

CHAPTER 4

Damien Chance - Bolivia Beginnings

I FIRST came to Bolivia as part of a small gold mining operation, working for a group of investors who hired me for my background in scuba diving and security work. Their plan was for me to help train the local natives to work with the underwater dredging equipment, and to keep an eye on their investment. I'm pretty sure they gave me the job because nobody else wanted it. The project was running out of money, so the pay was lousy, and the living conditions were rough. But for me, it was an opportunity for a little paid adventure, and at the time, that's exactly what I needed.

When I first arrived in Bolivia, all I knew about the country, the people, and the culture, was what I'd read in a few travel guides. I didn't know more than a handful of words in Spanish when I first climbed off the plane, but figured I could survive as long as I carried my Spanish/English dictionary around in my hip pocket. The locals began referring to it as "*mi Biblia*" — my Bible, because I constantly referred to it for guidance.

My deal with the investors was straightforward, consisting of a small salary and a piece of the profits. Of course, I had the same hopes of finding that ever-elusive mother lode that every adventurer dreams of. More importantly, I came to find myself. I was ready for some serious changes in life and thought this might be the way to find out what kind of man I really was.

Back in the States I'd spent most of my professional life in the suit-and-tie crowd, subscribing to what I believed, or at least what I was always told, was the "normal route" — the nine-to-five corporate regimen. Truth be told, I was damn good at it, but it wasn't the real me. When I finally got fed up with what I believed to be the hypocritical world of big business, I dropped out.

I once heard that a rut was nothing more than a grave with both ends kicked out, and I was tired of living in a rut, so I took a job working as a bouncer in one of the toughest nightclubs in town. It was an entirely different lifestyle than what I was used to, and most of the people who knew me thought I'd lost my mind, but it was just the change I needed to kick things in a new direction.

A friend of mine introduced me to a man who was looking for someone to launch off on a pie-in-the-sky adventure down to the middle of nowhere in the Amazon basin. Since I never was much for vicarious living, and would rather chase a dream than watch someone else do it on some mindless reality television show, it sounded like the perfect opportunity. With six-hundred-and-twenty bucks in my pocket, the fire of adventure burning in my gut, and a one-way ticket, I quit my job, packed my bags, and left for Bolivia.

Less than three months into the project the results were much less than what the investors were hoping for, and the money began drying up. Since I'd spent most of my time in camp and saved a big part of the small salary I'd been paid so far, I had enough to scrape by a little longer on my own. I wasn't ready to toss in the towel and go back to the States, so I made an offer to the owners that if they'd let me use their equipment, I'd pay the daily operating expenses out of whatever gold we found, and they could send down new investors to look at the operation while it was up and running. At least that way they'd have a chance to sell their assets instead of just abandoning them in the jungle. With nothing to lose, they agreed, and I bought myself a little more time in the Amazon.

The best way to keep things going was to make a deal with some of the locals who had been working for me in camp. They agreed to stay on for food and a piece of whatever gold we found. Times were tough in this part of the world, and they didn't have many other options, so we were in business.

After a few months of hand-to-mouth operations, one evening I piled the crew into the jeep and headed to town for a little R&R. More importantly, I was planning to meet with a prospective new investor coming down from Texas.

It was a two-hour drive to Chulumani, and in most places the winding old road was little more than a heavily rutted cattle trail. We could have walked straight up the side of the mountain and been there in just under an hour, but hell, it was Saturday night, and trudging through the thick, humid jungle would have taken all the fun out of it.

I dropped my crew off in the plaza and drove up Calle Junin toward La Hosteria, the only decent hotel in town. Decent meaning that they changed the sheets on a regular basis, had private showers in some of the rooms, and locks on the doors that worked. Twelve dollars a night and first-class accommodations for this part of the world.

I was so excited about the possibility of having new money pumped into the project that I sprinted up the steep wooden steps, taking them two at a time all the way up to the third floor. I rapped on the door while whistling to myself and was utterly shocked by the man who answered.

Gerald Parker looked like a test dummy for Gucci adventure wear, covered in khaki from head to toe. His ensemble included heavily starched khaki pants, a long sleeve khaki shirt, and a leather bush vest covered with mesh pockets and zippers. And of course, he had on a pair of heavy leather boots that were polished to a brilliant sheen, and a wide brimmed safari hat. I couldn't resist reaching over and flicking the bright orange tag that dangled off the back of his hat.

"You might want to clip that thing off before you go out," I suggested. "It probably wouldn't be a good idea to advertise that you paid more for your hat than most of the people around here make in a month."

He reached up and felt the tag, yanked it loose, and flicked it to the floor.

"I'm Chance, and it's nice to meet you," I said, extending my hand.

"I'm Gerald Parker," he said, gripping my hand and shaking it like he was trying to prime a pump. "Damn nice to meet you. Been hearing lots of good things about you and it's good to be here, but how do you stand all this heat? It's hotter than hell and this bed is going to be like sleeping on a pile of old rags. And how do you deal with all these Mexicans?" He was rambling like a man with nine days of work to do and only two days to get it done. He sucked in a breath like he was about to start again, so I reached over and laid my hand on his shoulder, trying to calm him down a bit.

"First of all, Mr. Parker, they aren't Mexicans. We're a little farther south than that. They're Bolivians, and…"

"Hell, they all look the same to me," he bellowed, cutting me off in mid-sentence and laughing at his narrow-minded observation.

"Be that as it may, we might get along better if we just stick with calling them Bolivians, okay?"

"You got it, son!" He was still talking loud enough to be heard two blocks away. "And quit calling me Mr. Parker. Just call me Gerald, or Parker, or boss, or what do they call it down here? *Jefe* — yeah, that's it, you can just call me *jefe*."

I cringed. "How about we just stick with Parker for now?"

"You got it!"

"And the heat won't bother you as much if you'll ditch that heavy leather vest and slip on a T-shirt," I suggested. "After all, we are in a sub-tropical region here."

"Oh, hell no! This outfit cost me an arm and a leg. Besides, it's what all the big-time adventurers are wearing these days.

"Whatever you think," I said, shaking my head. "Now, if you'd like, we can sit down and talk about what's going on in camp and the real potential for this project." I pulled a folded sheaf of papers out of my hip pocket. I'd been working on the operating numbers and projections for over a week.

"Whoa, son! Just hold your horses." He stepped back deeper into the room and held up his hand. His new leather boots squeaked on the wood plank floor. "We can talk about business tomorrow. Tonight, let's drink some of the local firewater and chase some *señoritas*. Hell, I bet they're going to love the new *jefe* in town. Whatcha' say, partner? Let's party!"

All I wanted to do was get down to business. Plus, I'd promised my crew that we'd have a nice sit-down dinner and enjoy something we didn't have to hunt and kill first and wasn't served up on a pointed stick. But, Gerald Parker, as obnoxious as he might be, was the best hope we had to keep the operation going until we hit real pay dirt, so I bit my lip, and said, "Sure, let's go show you around town."

• • •

I took Parker over to the *teatro* — the town dance hall. Bolivians love celebrating holidays and it seemed like they had something marked on the calendar at least once a month. This one was the *Fiesta de San Juan*. For some damn reason the festivities included starting little bonfires all over the place, and I knew the whole valley would be filled with smoke by morning. And just like every year, at least a dozen old shacks would end up burned to the ground. Liquor, loud music, and dancing — the three main ingredients for any successful Bolivian festival.

By the time we got to the *teatro* the party was already in full swing. I could see my crew had given up on having a nice sit-down dinner with us and were at least a case and a half of beer along the road to having a really good time. I motioned toward their table to make sure they could see that I was with the investor. Cristina was also there. She smiled, winked, and blew me a kiss, reminding me of what made me the happiest these days.

Cristina was a beautiful young woman who I'd met shortly after I first arrived in Chulumani. She didn't speak much English, but had an endless supply of patience for me to fumble through "*mi Biblia*" so we could communicate, and we were building an amazing relationship together. I adored her simple and sincere ways, and for the first time in my life, felt like I was with a woman who cared about me for *who* I was, and not who she thought she could change me into. I was tired of women always trying to *fix* me, and Cristina was turning out to be exactly what I'd always dreamed of.

Parker wasted no time becoming a serious partaker of the local brew and quickly began showing his true colors. It wasn't a pretty sight. Under the heavy mental fog of too much beer, and feeling his newfound bravado, he began preaching his distaste for the drug business and his belief that the root of the entire problem was right here in Bolivia. Then, to make sure that everyone could hear is drunken opinions, he climbed up on the stage.

I walked out of the restroom at the far end of the building just in time to see his presentation begin. I looked over to my crew, wondering why in the hell they hadn't tried to stop him. They looked back and shrugged their collective shoulders, giving me a sort of "what could we do" response.

"Hey!" Parker yelled, swinging a half-empty bottle of Paceña beer over his head. When that got no response, he screamed even louder. "Hey, I said!" He threw the bottle against the wall, showering beer and broken glass over the crowd. The music stopped. "Don't you morons know that the whole damn drug problem starts right here with all you Mexicans? If y'all would quit growing all this coca and get yourselves some *real* jobs, we wouldn't have such a problem back in the good old U...S...A!" He slurred his words, believing that if he talked really slow, and really loud, somehow, he would magically overcome the language barrier. Nobody had a clue what he was ranting about, but they knew he was a drunken *gringo* that was pissed-off about something. The part about "all you Mexicans" just sailed right over their heads. More importantly, he was stomping on a lot of local toes.

A few years back, a contingent of law enforcement officers rolled into town with the primary purpose of eradicating the local coca fields. Tragically, they underestimated the value the people around Chulumani put on their coca plants.

The night of their arrival, deep asleep in what they believed to be a peaceful town they could easily manipulate, a mob stormed into their rooms and dragged them out into the street. They beat them into submission with axe handles and lengths of bamboo. Then, without the benefit of due process of law, they were immediately judged guilty and summarily slaughtered. Their bodies were hacked into bloody quarters and hung on display throughout the town as a macabre warning. Local justice was swift, sure, and deadly in this part of the world.

After that night, nobody would dare speak of what had taken place, and the vigilante attackers were never identified or brought to trial. And even though government sponsored eradication took place all over the rest of the country, the short coca bushes that grew on the terraced hillsides near Chulumani were off limits.

These simple villagers didn't produce or tolerate the use of drugs. For them, the coca plant was sacred — an integral part of their Inca heritage. It had been used in religious ceremonies, medicinal concoctions, and chewed to stave off hunger and thirst for hundreds of years. They weren't about to stand by and watch their culture destroyed because people in other countries couldn't control their own addictive appetites.

Now, here was someone else, ranting and raving about the evils of coca and swinging the club of judgment. I knew what Parker was doing was much more than stupid. It was suicidal — for all of us.

I could feel the tension brewing and was certain that a violent confrontation was close at hand, so I quickly corralled Parker and my crew into the jeep and began the long drive back to camp. There was no doubt in my mind that he would be safer spending the night with us than risking it alone in town. So much for a peaceful night of R&R.

Cristina sat beside me in the jeep. Even though we lived together in camp, I'd tried to talk her into staying in town with her family tonight. I thought it would be safer considering what Parker had stirred up, but she wouldn't hear of it. She was "my woman", and around here that designation didn't carry the negative social connotations that it did back in the States. It was something she was proud of, and she believed that her place was by my side, no matter what.

I pulled up to the edge of camp and watched as the crew wrestled Parker into one of the empty huts. He was still drunk, ranting about his political opinions and flexing his beer muscles.

"Just dump him on a cot and let him sleep it off. He may be a royal pain in the ass, but he's our pain in the ass, and he might be the only hope we've got left to keep things going around here," I said.

I walked over to the lone sentry, making sure that all was secure for the night. Then, I took Cristina by the hand and we headed to our hut.

The life we shared in camp was about as simple as it could possibly be. We lived in a one room, dirt floor, thatch-roofed bamboo hut.

She helped me learn the ways of her people, and I tried to show her what it was like to have a man who truly loved her. I was happier than I'd ever been, and I believed that she was, too.

Cristina knew I was upset about what happened in the *teatro*, so she snuggled close and rubbed her hand along the path of my spine, kneading out the tension and trying to help me relax. I smiled, knowing that I truly did have the woman I had always dreamed of.

"*Te amo*," I whispered into the night.

"I love you, too," she replied. She might not know much English, but she'd learned the words that mattered the most.

There was a sliver of moonlight shining through our thatched roof, bathing us in a heavenly glow, and I definitely felt blessed.

We'd only been asleep for a few hours when I was abruptly kicked into awareness by the unnerving sounds of screams and gunshots barreling down the trail. Instinctively, I rolled out of bed, pulling on a pair of shorts and yanking a T-shirt over my head. I grabbed the cut-down 12-gauge shotgun I always kept close at hand and pushed through the multi-colored plastic sheet that served as our front door. Cristina was right on my heels.

As I racked a shell into the chamber, I couldn't believe what I was seeing. Less than a hundred meters up the trial there were at least fifty men carrying flaming torches and waving clubs. A handful of them were firing rifles into the air. I roughly translated what they were screaming as, "Death to the *gringo!*"

"Shit!" I started mentally running through our options.

Panic threw a strong-arm grip over camp and the crew gathered around our hut for protection. I knew that a bamboo hut was the last place they should be seeking refuge from blazing torches and gunfire. I'd tried to teach them that in case of an emergency like this, they should scatter into the surrounding jungle for cover, and then make their way to the safety of town once they knew everyone was okay. Unfortunately, sometimes the best laid plans go straight to hell as soon as the first shots are fired.

The angry mob swarmed into camp, firing wildly and torching anything that would burn. I began pumping round after 12-gauge round into the attackers, watching as my shots knocked one after the other from life into a violent and bloody death. I was living through it all like a slow-motion movie. Every vivid detail was exaggerated, and death and destruction were playing the starring roles. Then, the lights went out.

• • •

When I finally started coming around, the sun was peeking over the mountains and there was a heavy blanket of mist hovering just above the surface of the river. I was chilled to the bone and felt like I'd been cracked in the head with an axe handle, which I soon found out was exactly what had happened. It took several agonizing moments to clear my vision and gather my thoughts, and then I struggled up to a standing position. I quickly began to realize that what I'd thought was some horrible nightmare, was in fact, an even more tragic reality.

I looked around at what was left of our camp, trying to soak in the gruesome sight. There was nothing but smoldering ashes and mangled bodies scattered around like useless refuse. Most of the victims had been hacked and burned beyond recognition, but I knew who they were. They were my friends — my family.

Dear God, I thought, taking in the unimaginable brutality. *Why? They were only trying to make a few dollars to feed their families.* My stomach wretched violently, and then the other ugly shoe of reality dropped. *Cristina. Where was Cristina?*

My footing was unsteady because of the savage blow I'd taken to the head, but I began frantically searching through the carnage for what I feared I'd find. Then, I saw her.

Cristina was laid out at the edge of the river, face up, her head surrounded by a dark halo of blood-soaked earth. Her throat had been slashed and her clothes torn away. It was painfully obvious that she'd been beaten, raped, and then killed. A tidal wave of nausea washed over me. I dropped to one knee, looking into the hollow stare of her lifeless eyes, and felt my heart shatter.

I slipped off my shirt and laid it gently over her face. Then, I pulled her torn nightgown up around her frail body, trying to give her some dignity. I held her cold hand and felt completely empty. The woman I had always dreamed of was gone.

A lone cry broke into my misery.

"Help me! Somebody, please help me!"

The plea was coming from somewhere close by, hidden in the cover of jungle, and I realized the cries for help were in English.

"Parker!" I grabbed the charred handle of a machete lying nearby and ran toward the pleading voice.

I found him lying face down on the ground, wearing nothing but a pair of soiled underwear. His pale skin was speckled with hundreds of red welts that he'd gotten from a night of exposure to ravenous jungle insects.

"Are you hurt?" I reached down and carefully rolled him over onto his back. I could see he wasn't injured, but scared and in shock.

"It was horrible, just horrible!" He was blubbering uncontrollably like a terrified child. "They were running around and screaming and shooting and burning everything in sight. And that girl. Oh, my God, that poor girl."

What he said about "that girl" sent a stabbing chill through me. I grabbed a handful of his matted hair and yanked him up to a sitting position. "What do you mean, what they did to that girl?"

"It was horrible, just horrible," he said again. Sobs racked his body and he spat out his words in short, emotional jolts.

"You saw what they were doing to her? You saw it and didn't do a goddamn thing to help?" Red hot hanger raced through my veins, blurring my vision with rage. "What in the hell is the matter with you? What kind of man are you?"

"I was scared, man. And who in the hell do you think you are talking to me like that?" He jerked loose from my grip, wiping his forearm across his face and smearing tears and dirt into streaks of mud. "I saw those crazy bastards shooting and burning everything in sight and I ran into the bush — that's what the hell I did." He was regaining his composure and elitist attitude.

I glanced over and saw a mud-caked Ruger .357 revolver lying on the ground. "How many shots did you get off with your pistol?" I tipped my chin toward the gun.

"Shots? Are you nuts? I didn't want those killers to know where I was," he snapped. He realized that the danger was over, and the more he talked, the more he got back into full swing as the arrogant *gringo*. "They weren't my problem, and neither was that cute little piece of ass they were passing around like their own private party favor."

I glared down at him, and for the briefest moment almost felt sorry for a man so self-centered that he could watch others being slaughtered, and an innocent young woman violated and killed, and not lift a hand to help. Then, I saw him for the worthless coward that he really was, hiding in the darkness like a little bitch.

"That woman you watched them rape and kill was *my* woman, and you're nothing but a worthless piece of scum that..."

"Whoa, son, you can't talk to me..."

The emotions of all that had happened erupted within me. I stepped up and fired-off a kick with all the power I could muster, slamming my foot square into his head. He flopped over onto his back like a sack of wet trash.

With Parker lying unconscious in the bush, I walked back over to Cristina's body. I looked around until I found a shovel and began digging her grave. There was no way that I would ever let her family see what had really happened to her. All I wanted to do now was to make sure she had a peaceful place to rest, right here by the river where we'd shared that once in a lifetime love.

CHAPTER 5

"*MĒSTER Chance, Mēster Chance! Por favor, Mēster Chance!*"

I bolted upright at the pleading and incessant banging on my door. I rolled out of bed, shirtless, still wearing the faded jeans I'd laid down in last night. As irritating as it was, I was glad for the intrusion. At least it brought me back from my dark dreams. I snatched the pistol off the nightstand and slipped it into the waistband at the small of my back.

"Yeah, yeah, okay, I'm coming." I stepped over and opened the door.

"*Mēster Chance,*" the boy pleaded. "*Teléfono, larga distancia, rapido!*"

Even though it was rare for this part of country, the hotel in Chulumani had a landline that worked — at least most of the time. Now, I understood why little Josè was so agitated and what all the racket was about. A long-distance call usually brought really good news, or really bad news. Either way, it was cause for excitement.

"Watch my room, *mi amigo.*" I reached down into my pocket and pulled out a wad of *bolivianos*, pressing them into the boy's palm. I wasn't sure how much money I'd just given him, but if it was more than five bucks, it was more than he made in a week running errands around the hotel. I knew he'd walk home tonight with a little more pride in his step and unselfishly share the bounty with his poor family.

I padded barefoot down the hallway to the old black rotary phone. When I picked up the receiver, the tangled cord almost dragged the whole thing off onto the floor. Reflexes kicked in when I grabbed for it and I stubbed my toe on the bottom of the heavy wooden desk.

"Son...of...a...yeah, hello!"

A distant voice crackled over the poor connection. It was a voice that delighted the little demons that haunted my conscience.

"How's life in the boonies, buddy?"

I tensed. It damn sure wasn't any old friend. So much for the good news option.

"Not bad," I said flatly. My toe throbbed and I tried rubbing it against the heel of my other foot for relief.

"You do know who this is, don't you?"

"Yeah, I know who it is." I couldn't imagine what Don Taylor wanted with me now.

"I'm going to be in La Paz in a couple of days. How about we get together?"

"What do you want?" I wasn't in the mood for any chit-chat and doubted meeting with the man was going to do anything but drag my life further into the muck.

"We can meet at the same place we did last time. How about Wednesday, at midnight?"

"Why?" I persisted.

The connection went dead.

A call from Don Taylor could only mean one thing. Bad news.

I shuffled back down the hallway, stopping briefly to tousle the perpetually tangled mop of thick black hair on José's head. The little ten-year-old was grinning from ear to ear, standing proud and guarding my room like the most vigilant of soldiers.

"Alright, run on down and get me a ticket for tomorrow morning's bus to La Paz." I saw the glazed look of confusion in his eyes. I guess helping him with his English lessons hadn't been so effective after all. *"Quiero viajar a La Paz en la manana. Comprar mi una boleto, por favor."*

"Si, Mēster Chance!" His eyes lit up like Christmas morning. Being able to brag to his friends that he worked for the only *gringo* in town was like some adolescent status symbol.

I pulled out my wallet and counted off enough money for the ticket and another little bonus. He sprinted off and I could hear him singing as he bounded down the stairs and out into the street.

My mind raced through the possibilities of what Don Taylor might want with me this time. None of them were pleasant thoughts.

CHAPTER 6

D ON Taylor walked up the corridor to the Jefferson Memorial. He wore a heavy camelhair overcoat with the collar turned up high on his neck. His gloved hands were thrust deep into his pockets and he shivered at the bitter cold. Washington D.C. could be an absolute bitch in winter.

Taylor's job had no official title. He didn't carry embossed business cards and didn't have a fancy office with an attractive secretary to greet his clients, carry on small talk, or offer them an espresso. He didn't exist in the traditional sense. He had no social security number — at least not a real one. He paid no taxes, and his name and fingerprints didn't show up in any government, military, or law enforcement databases. He was what the old guard referred to as a "ghost" — one of a handful of elite operatives that handled assignments for the few remaining clandestine agencies that survived all the budget cuts and political correctness adjustments over the last few administrations.

Government hierarchy from the President on down denied the existence of men like Taylor. It didn't make the general public feel all warm and fuzzy when details of how he got his assignments handled hit the ten o'clock news. If an operation went sour and resulted in undesirable political backlash, men like him were simply labeled as renegades from the past who were operating on their own. They were tossed out and left for the media wolves to devour — tasty tidbits and cannon fodder for the nightly news. However, when the political burners flared up hot enough to singe a few highly placed bureaucratic butts, and conventional methods didn't garner the necessary results, he was always provided the intel and funding he needed to get things resolved.

Taylor was the quintessential soldier. He asked few questions and made no judgments. He followed orders given and absolutely nothing got in the way of him seeing that they were carried out. And when his assignments were completed, he took their money without any challenge of conscience. He'd overcome that obstacle too many years ago to even remember.

Taylor had served his country proudly in the military and was recruited after this third tour of duty. When he agreed to their terms, an unrecognizable body was shipped back to the States in a sealed coffin draped in the American flag. A sympathetic letter was sent to what little family he had, thanking them for his service and sacrifice, and telling them he'd been killed while fighting bravely in action. From that day forward he carried out his service as a "living ghost". He often wondered what it would have been like if he'd made a different choice for his life. What would have happened if he'd chosen to come home "alive". But those thoughts were old dark water long passed under the bridge of life. He knew there were too many hard miles behind him now to begin having second thoughts about what "might have been". Regrets were something a man like Don Taylor could not afford to have.

He saw a lone orange eye glowing in the darkness a few yards up the walkway and knew the man he'd come to meet was waiting. He'd already caught a whiff of what smelled like burnt coffee and cinnamon and was certain that his old friend was puffing on a Nicaraguan *El Padron* cigar. It was his favorite smoke and one of the few pleasurable vices the old warhorse still allowed himself.

"Good evening, Mr. Taylor." The man's graveled voice resonated in the cold night air.

"General, it's good to see you. You know, I've got some connections that can get you some good Cuban cigars if you'd like." Taylor knew what the response was going to be and fought back a grin in anticipation.

"Cubans! I wouldn't smoke a goddamned Cuban cigar if it was served up between Marilyn Monroe's tits."

Taylor smiled.

"Fucking Castro. We should have jammed a grenade up his ass back in the 60s when we had the chance."

"Well, he's gone now and…"

"Have you contacted your man?" he said, cutting Taylor off and getting right to the point.

"Yes, sir. I'm meeting with him in two days."

"Will he do the job?" The general rubbed a calloused hand across his stiff gray flat top. It was the same haircut he'd had since his days dodging bullets in the trenches with the rest of the grunts, over fifty years ago. He was a soldier to the core, and always subscribed to the practice of leading from the front.

"I have no doubt, sir," Taylor assured him.

"Let's hope so," he said.

It was no secret that the general was apprehensive about Taylor's choice of operatives for this assignment. He pulled a long drag off his cigar and blew out a thick cloud of heavy gray smoke that hung in the frigid night air. He reached inside his overcoat and removed an envelope. He tapped the edge several times to the palm of his hand like he was contemplating his decision, and finally handed it over. He was old school and believed that a job like this wasn't one where you'd want to leave an electronic trail of evidence to be ferreted out by people looking to cover their asses if things went sideways — which they often did.

Handwritten intel and the flare of a match to erase the evidence. It was the only way to go.

Taylor was aware of the general's reservations about his choice of operatives. But the problem was, the entire force of elite spec-op units was already spread paper thin and committed to other actions around the globe, with most of them deployed to conflicts in various Middle East locales. Of course, there were several decent mercenary organizations out there, but most of their ranks were making piles of cash pulling triggers in that same theater of operations. Since all indications were that those ongoing battles were going to be long, drawn out affairs, that left the pool for young spec-op candidates bone dry — especially the ones who would agree to dance completely outside the boundaries of conventional military and governmental structure. Bottom line: The war on drugs was left sucking hind tit.

As much as he hated to admit it, Taylor knew he'd edged past his prime for carrying out the kind of hands-on field work a job like this required. It was time to recruit some new blood into the game. He just had to be more creative about where he found it. He knew most of the wannabe jerk-offs who got a hard-on reading *Soldier of Fortune* magazine and paid ridiculous sums of money to attend weekend combat courses, didn't know the difference between a Ranger and Rambo. He needed the real deal and believed that Chance might be just the ticket he'd been looking for.

Taylor looked straight into the steel-gray eyes of his old comrade in arms, and with absolute confidence, said, "Look, I know your concerns, but I believe this man is as good as any we could get from our old sources. He might not have the background and formal training we usually look for, but that doesn't mean he hasn't got the mettle and motivation to get it done."

"It's your ass if he fails," the general said, turning and walking toward his waiting car.

"Tell me something I don't already know," Taylor mumbled into the darkness.

CHAPTER 7

LISA Dalton's phone rang five times before she could answer it. She was standing just outside the bathroom door, dripping water on the bedroom carpet. She had one towel wrapped around her narrow waist, and another twisted around her head like an oversized turban holding up her wet hair. She cradled the phone in the crook of her neck and grabbed the television remote with her free hand. She hit the mute button and the room fell silent, but she could still see some intrepid traveler nibbling on grilled scorpions somewhere in Thailand. The "foodie shows" were her latest obsession. She often imagined jetting away with Alan to some exotic locale and trying foods they would wince about before eating, and then laughing together afterward at their adventurous culinary gusto.

"Hello!" She was short of breath after rushing to catch the call before it went to voicemail, but it wasn't because she was out of shape. It was nervous anticipation that had her heart racing, hoping it would be Alan.

She turned her body slightly to the left in order to get a better view in the floor-length mirror, appreciating all her hard work in the gym. Her breasts were full and firm and her legs long and toned. Her upper body tapered down to a narrow waist and a flat stomach, and then flared out to the curve of her hips, and what Alan liked to call her "apple ass". She was the epitome of sexy.

"Hey, sweetheart!" Breckenridge had just checked in to his room at the Plaza Hotel in downtown La Paz. After he'd tossed his suitcases on the bed, the first thing he did was call Lisa.

"I'm sorry you had to let it ring so many times," she said. "I was in the tub."

A sly grin crept across Breckenridge's face. "I wish I was there with you. I'd be happy to scrub your back."

Lisa played along with the banter. She dropped her voice down an octave, and in a husky whisper, said, "Darling, if you were here, you could do a *lot* more than scrub my back."

"Promises, promises," Breckenridge said, and they both laughed. He remembered their last little "tub session". Three days afterwards his knees were still so sore he could barely walk. "I just wanted to call and tell you that I love you, and that I'll be home in a few days. I'll try to call when I can, but you know how the phone service is down here."

"Please, be careful," Lisa said, thinking about some of the recent political developments in Bolivia. She remembered the last time Alan was in La Paz, there had been rioting and protests outside of his hotel and he'd barely made it to the airport for his flight out. She couldn't imagine that it was any safer now for a spit-and-shine businessman like him. As far as she knew, that's all Alan Breckenridge had ever been.

"Don't worry, darling. I'm always careful." He wanted to ease her mind as much as he could from six thousand miles away. "As soon as I get back, why don't we sneak off to one of those places you're always talking about. We can chow down on some boiled grub worms, or barbecued coyote, or whatever the hell is on top of the "adventure menu" these days. How does that sound?"

"How about some grilled scorpions? I just saw a great show about street food in Thailand and it looks amazing!" Lisa was beaming at the thought of the two of them getting away for a while.

"I'm in!" Breckenridge said. What he really wished was that he could cash in some of his chips and the two of them could just escape. Maybe find an exotic, non-extradition island where they could lie in the sun, sip colorful tropical drinks, and make love to the rhythm of the waves breaking on the beach. That's what he wished for, but he knew it was nothing more than a pipe dream. As long as he was under the thumb of J. Edward Adams III, he would never have any semblance of a normal life.

"I'll put in for some time off and start checking prices for airline tickets and hotels," Lisa said. "I love you, Alan. Don't you ever forget that."

"I know you do, sweetheart. I love you, too. See you in a few days." Breckenridge hung up the phone, and then walked over to pull closed the heavy floor-to-ceiling drapes. He didn't have any interest in seeing the twinkling lights of the city dance across the skyline of La Paz. He began unpacking his bags. What he was really doing was procrastinating, doing anything he could to delay contacting the man he'd come to see. He already had a monster of a headache and his nerves were worn ragged. His stomach felt like a bucket full of angry eels, and he knew it was all just a small taste of what was yet to come.

CHAPTER 8

DON Taylor stood next to his packed bags at the front door of his small apartment and made the call.

"Sergeant Blevins," the man answered. Taylor had dialed a direct number to one of the flight operations desks.

"Good evening, Sergeant. This is Don Taylor. Will you connect me, please?" Taylor's arrangements at the base were so when he called the operations desk, they had standing orders to immediately patch him through to one of the spec-ops hangers.

"Yes, sir, Mr. Taylor. One moment, please." The young sergeant didn't know who, or what, Don Taylor was, but he knew when he was on base, he was given wide berth and treated with a great deal of respect. He also knew anyone treated with that much regard that didn't wear a uniform, was someone he didn't want to cross. Consequently, he handled the man with extreme care for his own peace of mind.

Taylor knew the DEA had several planes operating out of Andrews Air Force Base for their ongoing operations in South America. He hoped he'd be lucky enough to catch a ride down on one of their flights instead of having to go commercial.

"This is Captain Marklin. How can I help you this evening, Mr. Taylor?"

"I need a ride to Bolivia. SAM FOX got anything going down that way?" Taylor used the old air base moniker. The call sign stood for Special Air Mission (SAM), Foreign (FOX). In addition to having the primary task of handling flights for the President of the United States, Andrews was also responsible for providing flight services for the Vice President, the President's cabinet, members of Congress, military leaders, and other high-ranking dignitaries. He knew being located less than ten miles from D.C.'s power hub, they also handled some of the less publicized flight operations for the world's most powerful governmental machine.

"One moment, sir." Captain Marklin scanned the log. "There's a flight scheduled to leave at 0400. It has a couple of brief stops, but they're mostly touch-and-go pickups, so we can have you in La Paz by tomorrow evening."

"Outstanding! Snag me a seat and I'll be there in a few hours." He knew he'd be logged onto the flight by a number designation. No names. Anyone who didn't already know who he was, had no need to know. The DEA pilots had all been around long enough to know better than to ask unnecessary questions.

Taylor stood in the small foyer of his cramped apartment, looking around at the sparse furnishings. Rental center rejects, mostly, but he knew they were all he needed until what he referred to as his "escape to retirement", and "escape" was a spot-on description of what would take place when that time came. Most men in his line of work never lived long enough to enjoy the fruits of their labors. He had a different plan.

Taylor learned something especially important many years ago: The more treacherous the business, the more they were willing to pay to have it handled.

Don Taylor had definitely handled of a lot of treachery in his career.

CHAPTER 9

J. EDWARD sat in a button-tufted wing chair in the study of his home. He lived in an exclusive enclave tucked away within the borders of Oklahoma City. It was an old money haven. New money bought ostentatious mansions in the suburbs north of town, but he wanted to be associated with the aristocratic flavor that came with riches steeped in tradition, not the luck of the dot.com stock market lottery.

Even though his palatial mansion had cost him over twenty-five-million-dollars, he still considered it beneath what he believed he deserved. He knew once all his plans were in place, he'd move out of this "cow town", as he often referred to it, and go back to the East Coast where he believed he rightly belonged.

He gazed into the roaring fireplace, feeling the heat tighten the skin across his face as he contemplated his impending ascent into greatness. He was already worth hundreds of millions of dollars, but knew he had to be worth billions to accomplish his goals.

Drugs. At first, he questioned whether he should involve himself in such an enterprise at this stage in his life, but when he considered the tremendous profits to be made and how quickly he could acquire them, that tempered some of the distastefulness of the business. Besides, some of the great family fortunes in history were padded by dabbling in the liquor business back during prohibition, and those were certainly illegal pursuits at the time. He rationalized that his interests were no worse than theirs — just a different product of vice at a different time in history.

When he was vacationing in Majorca, Spain, J. Edward had been introduced to a man he was told would be the next major worldwide force in the cocaine business. A trusted associate had brought him to his private villa for a drink, and to discuss their common interests. He was also worth hundreds of millions of dollars, and made it clear that he wanted much more, and all the power that went along with it. J. Edward could certainly appreciate his ambitions.

So, that was it. J. Edward Adams III and Ramiro Dueñas became partners. Dueñas agreed to supply all the cocaine J. Edward could distribute, and at a price he couldn't possibly come close to anywhere else. As long as J. Edward continued to buy an enormous and continuous supply, Dueñas would produce and deliver it to him. The profit possibilities for both parties were staggering. J. Edward was so confident in their arrangement that he'd even given Dueñas a ten-million-dollar deposit to secure his first shipment.

And now, this mysterious security problem. Distributors were waiting. Promises had been made to unscrupulous associates, who much like J. Edward, did not respond kindly to excuses. More importantly, enormous piles of money were waiting to be raked in.

"Breckenridge," he mumbled toward the crackling fire. "You damn well better straighten this mess out."

He rubbed the misshapen old bullet that hung around his neck. Then, he reached down and kneaded the area around his right knee, trying to work the constant pain down to a tolerable level.

CHAPTER 10

I GOT off the bus in Villa Fatima, a vibrant neighborhood on the out-skirts of La Paz where buses and trucks unload passengers and cargo that come in from the surrounding countryside. As usual, I was covered with dust and smelled like the greasy *chorizo* the *cholita* who sat next to me nibbled on the entire trip.

I always enjoy the scenery on the road from Chulumani to La Paz because of the panoramic diversity. In the Sud Yungas, the tropical growth that lines the road is lush and green and fills the air with the aroma of dozens of varieties of flowers. As the bus follows the narrow ribbon of road higher up into the mountains, the terrain becomes as desolate as a lunar landscape, punctuated with steep rugged walls of dark stone with no visible signs of life. A little farther up into the alti-tudes of the Andean Pass, snow and ice cover the ground year-round. The trip is an experience in the contrasting diversities of nature in the span of just a few hours. The perilous road climbs from a beginning altitude in Chulumani of about twenty-five-hundred feet, to over fifteen thousand before it finally winds its way down into the thin mountain air of La Paz.

I remember going on a family vacation in Colorado when I was a kid. I thought the roads through the Rocky Mountains seemed treach-erous back then, but now, they seem like child's play. Most of the roads to the villages in this part of Bolivia cross extreme altitudes and are usually little more than one lane wide. The daring drivers maneuver them as if they're traveling on wide, paved highways. Dozens of buses and trucks go over the precipice each year, taking all their passengers with them. It's a violent and deadly ride to the end that the locals refer to as a "rollover".

"*Adios, amigo!*" I waved a grateful farewell to Enrique, the driver. I always try to catch his bus because I figure it gives me a better chance for survival.

"*Adios, don Chance!*" he yelled back, waving out the window as he ground the transmission down into the crawl gear, pulling back up the incline. The other passengers constantly berated him for driving so carefully, calling him *maricón* — homosexual. I appreciate is caution and believe anything I can do to avoid a "rollover ride" to the bottom of the valley is like money in the bank.

Standing on the corner, I waved toward traffic. Almost immediately, a battered old taxi slid up to the curb. I could hear the metal-on-metal grind of brakes worn past the point of safety.

"*El Prado. Hotel Copacabana, por favor,*" I said to the driver, sliding into the back seat. He nodded, jammed the shifter into first, and jerked away from the curb.

I stay at the Hotel Copacabana whenever I'm in La Paz. I've come to know the manager well and make sure to tip the bellboys and desk clerks generously. In return, they keep an eye on my room when I'm out, and if anyone comes around asking for me at the front desk, they look at them with a straight face, and ask, "Who?"

I'm a firm believer in the premise that a little extra caution goes a long way in the Third World. Just as important, the hotel has oversized tubs, thick absorbent towels, and hot water. After tepid showers at La Hosteria in Chulumani, and months of quick scrubs in the frigid Andean runoff waters in Rio Solocama, a soaking hot bath is like a dream come true. It constantly amazes me how valuable such simple pleasures in life have become.

The taxi rolled out of Villa Fatima, through the Miraflores District, and into the capital city of La Paz. There, on the edge of the city was the Parque Mirador, where I'd have my meeting with Don Taylor.

At the entrance to the park, street vendors sell everything from ice cream and candied apples to balloons and blow-up cartoon characters suspended on sticks. Families come in droves on weekends to enjoy cheap entertainment and to find a little reprieve from the misery most of them must endure on a daily basis, trying to scratch out a living in one of the poorest countries in South America.

There isn't much to do in the park, but up several levels of wide stone stairs there's a plateau that has some picnic tables and a few old metal slides for the kids. If you're as poor as most of the people living in El Alto, the neighborhood surrounding the high edge of the city, it doesn't take much to beat staying home and watching the gaping economic gulf between the haves and the have-nots grow continually wider. Bottom line: Hope is in short supply.

I thought about the contrast between the happy families I saw going into the park and the misery that would probably be bred there as a result of my meeting with Don Taylor. Once again, those little gremlins began dancing around in my conscience. I thought back to the first time I met Don Taylor, and how dramatically that meeting had changed my life. Memory lane isn't always such a pleasant road to travel.

CHAPTER 11

Damien Chance & Don Taylor -
The First Encounter

'D been back in Oklahoma for about six months. Since the massacre in camp that took the lives of Cristina and my crew, I'd crawled deep within myself. My grief felt smaller here, and for the time being, I preferred the emotional security of my own company.

I'd gone back to working as a bouncer at the Stone Horse Club. Lost in the crowd, the music, and the smoke, all I had to worry about was doing my job, which meant watching my ass and covering the backs of the men I worked with.

The local authorities in Bolivia had decided that there was no way for them to find out who was responsible for the attack on our camp — other than the men I'd "identified" with my 12-gauge. In typical South American fashion, they buried the dead and went on with life.

The Stone Horse is a holdover from the 80s — a relic in the new era of hip-hop and R&B clubs. They don't sell imported beer, mojitos, appletinis, or whatever the hell the flavor of the month is. Beer and shots are what keep the regulars liquored-up and happy. The music is hard core rock and roll and blares out of the sound system with enough force to rattle the fillings in your teeth. Big screen televisions hang down from the ceiling on heavy chains and run loops of music videos featuring buxom, gyrating women wearing just enough clothing to beat being classified as porn. The videos run without sound since it doesn't match the music being played on the dance floor, but nobody complains. It's funny how tits overshadow taste. There's a five-dollar cover charge at the door and a dress code that dictates shirts, pants, and shoes. Free, watered-down beer is served in plastic cups until ten o'clock. By then, nobody gives a damn what they're drinking.

The Stone Horse isn't the kind of place where it's a good idea to serve anything in glass bottles. The rationale being that if you're not going to let them in the front door with a weapon, why put one in their hands after they get in. On any given Friday or Saturday night, blue collar regulars pack the place to have a good time after a long week of having their noses to the grindstone. It's loud, wild, and just the kind of place I needed to try and keep my mind off of what happened down in Bolivia.

I leaned up against one of the eight long bars situated around the inside of the club, surveying the crowd. What had my interest now was a particularly stunning long-legged beauty in an electric blue lykra mini skirt. Mike, the club manager, sidled up next to me. He had to scream to be heard over the music.

"Damn, Chance, looks like two monkeys fuckin' in a sack!" He was referring to the girl's surgically enhanced breasts, bouncing around unfettered in her white lace spaghetti top. I smiled and nodded an affirmative response.

I like Mike. He always gives me work when I need it. It's a good deal for me and an even better deal for the club. He knows I'm more than the typical muscle-bound ne'er-do-well that generally gravitates toward working as a bouncer in a place like this. I know how to talk people out the door nine times out of ten, and when those instances arise where talk won't get it done, I can snag-and-drag a belligerent drunk as well as anyone in the business.

The enticing dancer continued her gyrations. We locked eyes. She swayed seductively with the rhythm of the music and began rubbing her hands across her ample bosom. Her short skirt rode up even higher on her shapely thighs.

"Makes my dick harder than Chinese arithmetic," Mike said, keeping his eyes on the show.

"Yeah, and it looks like she might be interested in some private math lessons," I laughed.

It was all just friendly bar banter between us. I had a hard and fast rule to never go home with a girl from the club. If you do, and it doesn't work out, then you'll be back here working, and she'll be right here in your face giving you a hard time. It's not worth the headache.

As Mike and I considered the erotic possibilities, a call blasted over the PA system, overriding the music.

"Security, bar six! Security, bar six!"

All eight bars in the club are numbered. When there's trouble, one of the bartenders can flip a switch that lights up a panel in the DJ booth, indicating the bar nearest the ruckus. The DJ announces it over the sound system and summons the bouncers.

I moved quickly through the crowd, jumping over chairs and pushing aside dancers. Some of the regulars could see what was happening and started chanting, "Chance, Chance, Chance!" This isn't the type of crowd that calls in the human rights lawyers when something goes down. They actually enjoy the spectacle of a good old-fashioned ass-kicking when someone deserves it.

When I got near bar six, I could see there wasn't a fight or any of the usual commotion. No blood or broken noses. That was the good news. The bad news was that there were two sour-looking men in cheap suits who'd bullied their way into the club. As I got closer, I could hear the doorman screaming over the music. "I don't give a damn who you are! You don't pay the five-buck cover charge, you don't get in!"

I had to laugh. Here were two guys that reeked of being cops, and the doorman was hounding them about the cover charge. Good man!

I moved up next to the one causing the most commotion.

"What seems to be the problem?"

"Are you Damien Chance?" he asked, looking at me suspiciously.

"Yeah," I said.

"We need to talk."

"Like the man said, you don't pay, you don't dance." I turned to walk away, motioning for the doorman to escort them out.

As I moved back into the crowd, one of the "suits" reached over and grabbed me by the shoulder, yanking me around to face him. I instinctively swung with the motion, picking up momentum and spinning through my hips, driving up with power from my thighs and landing a sharp elbow strike square on his jaw. He dropped like a sack of doorknobs, crumpling to the floor in a pile of brown suit, starched white shirt, and patterned maroon tie. The other man stood there for a second, and then slid back the edge of his jacket, exposing a holstered pistol and the distinctive little badge carried by agents with the FBI.

I leaned down and grabbed one arm of the man on the floor. I looked up at his partner, and said, "Unless you want to leave him lying here in spilt beer and God knows what else, give me a hand." Together, we helped him out the front door and sat him on the sidewalk. I knelt down and gently slapped his face a few times to help bring him around.

"What in the hell do you want?" I asked.

Still dazed, the man shook his head a few times to shake out the cobwebs. He flashed me his badge.

"Already seen one of those," I said.

He bristled even more. "Special Agent Donaldson, FBI, and I should arrest your sorry ass for assaulting a federal officer!" He stood up and started brushing off his suit, glaring at me.

"How in the hell was I supposed to know you're a Fed? You didn't identify yourself, and then skipped through the front door like you owned the place. I don't know what it's like around your office, but you come strolling into a place like this and grab a man from behind, you're likely to get your teeth loosened."

"He's right, Donaldson. We didn't identify ourselves," the other agent said, breaking the tension.

I reached over and flicked a wet cigarette butt off the man's shoulder.

"We need to talk down at our office." He moved his jaw in slow chewing motions like he was trying to make sure it wasn't broken.

"Got a warrant?" I was getting irritated.

"A warrant? Do you think we need a fucking warrant?" Now, he was fuming.

"Probably not, but it's what everyone on TV always asks — thought I'd give it a shot," I said.

"Shit-head," he mumbled. He stopped rubbing his jaw, straightened his jacket, and readjusted the leather holster clipped to his belt.

"Look guys, I don't get out of here until around two-thirty, and you've seen what it's like in there. I can't leave my guys shorthanded. How about I come down tomorrow afternoon?" I leaned up against the metal siding of the front entrance. The club's huge neon sign buzzed loudly above us, casting an odd blue light on the two agents.

"No way," Agent Donaldson brayed. FBI offices as soon as you get off. And if you're not there, we'll be back with a warrant, funny man, and I'll personally cuff your sorry ass and drag you in myself."

"Come on, surely you can let me go home and get a little shut-eye, or at least clean up a little."

"As *soon* as you get off," he reiterated. He tossed one of his cards on the ground by my feet, and then he and the other agent walked off.

"What the hell was that all about?" Mike asked. He was standing just inside the door, watching what was going on. He held a ten-inch length of steel pipe that was packed with lead shot and wrapped in silver duct tape. He didn't know who the men were but was ready in case I needed backup.

"Damned if I know," I said. "Couple of Feds said they needed to talk to me down at their office."

"About what?" Mike handed the pipe to the doorman so he could put it back under the counter.

"Couldn't say for sure, but I knocked one on his ass." I smiled. "Told them I'd come by after work."

"You popped a cop?" Mike asked, incredulously.

"Forget about it," I said. "I'm sure it doesn't have anything to do with the club. Now, let's go find that sack-of-monkeys in the blue mini-skirt."

"Right behind you, professor," he laughed.

We flowed back into the boisterous club.

• • •

It was a little after 3:00 a.m. when I rang the buzzer at the downtown offices of the FBI. The night security guard opened the glass door and gave me a thorough once-over. I know I must have looked rough. I smelled like smoke and all the beer that had been spilled, or thrown on me, at the club. My shirt had one sleeve ripped loose, compliments of a dedicated patron who wasn't ready to go home when we turned up the lights at closing time. There was a dark red bloodstain on my collar. It wasn't my blood.

"Whaddaya' want, slick?" The old night watchman smelled like tuna and I knew I'd probably interrupted his snack-in-a-sack.

"I'm here to see Frick and Frack with the FBI."

"Yeah, Agent Donaldson said you'd be coming by. Frick and Frack — I like that," he chuckled. "Come on in. Fifteenth floor."

"Thanks, chief. And sorry to bother you."

"That's okay. Needed to take a piss, anyway."

I walked past the security station on my way to the elevator and saw the muted glow from his portable black and white television. There was a half-eaten sandwich lying by an open bag of potato chips on the desk.

When the elevator doors slid open, my first impression of the FBI offices was exactly what I'd expected. Institutionalized. Gray metal desks, gray metal filing cabinets, and the walls were painted a depressing shade of dingy white. A handful of burnt orange plastic chairs that looked like rejects from a high school cafeteria were scattered around the waiting area. Fluorescent lights hummed in the ceiling and there was an American flag on a brass pole in one corner, and a portrait of the President of the United States to the right of a bullet-proof glass partition where a receptionist probably sat during normal business hours.

"Frick and Frack? You think that's funny, shit-bird?" The security guard must have called up to announce my arrival. Agent Donaldson was waiting for me. He had about as much personality as a cat turd. His jaw was starting to swell along with the bruising.

"Shit-head, shit-bird. You ever think about broadening your vocabulary? Maybe ask Santa for a thesaurus this year?" I asked. He didn't smile.

"Come on in and have a seat," he said, holding back the door to the inner offices. "Want coffee?" A real charmer.

"Yeah, thanks," I said. "But what I'd really like, is to know what this is all about. You saw the crowd that hangs out at the Stone

Horse. Having a couple of feds come in asking for me isn't the highest of recommendations."

"Well, wouldn't that be too bad if we've marred your sterling reputation," he smirked.

"Actually, knocking you on your ass probably offset any damage to my community standing."

He glared right through me. I got the distinct impression there wasn't going to be any love lost between us.

"That's right, Chance. It probably didn't hurt your reputation at all."

The voice came from behind me, and I spun around to see who'd joined us.

This newcomer looked to be just under six feet tall but had the aura of a much bigger man. He had close-cropped salt and pepper hair and deep experience lines that etched his tanned face. He wore a loose-fitting expensive suit, and I sensed a lean, powerful body that had been well maintained over the years. Quick assessment of your opponent comes with the territory of working as a bouncer, and I knew this man would be a formidable adversary. What struck me most were his eyes. They were as black as coal and had that deep, faraway look of someone who'd seen too many things in a lifetime that a man shouldn't have to see. I'd heard the old combat veterans refer to it as "The Thousand Yard Stare". He handed me my coffee. Styrofoam cup, of course. At least it wasn't gray.

"Chance, my name is Don Taylor." He shook my hand with a confident grip, and I could feel the rough callouses across his palm. This was no pencil pusher.

"Nice to meet you, Mr. Taylor." Although I'd taken an immediate dislike to the two FBI agents, I felt a natural ease with this man.

Taylor leaned back against the edge of the desk. He brushed his pant leg smooth and took a slow sip of coffee, giving Chance the once-over, making his own assessment.

"I was sorry to hear about what happened to your crew down in Bolivia, and especially about you girlfriend, Cristina. That was her name, wasn't it — Cristina?" He calmly took another sip of coffee.

What he said hit me like a brick. I sprung up out of my chair and slapped the cup out of his hand. Coffee splashed across the room.

"Who in the hell are you?" I demanded.

Taylor stayed calm — didn't move an inch, didn't twitch a muscle, and in a soft, calming tone, said, "Please, sit back down."

I sat back down, but mainly because the two FBI agents gripped the butts of their pistols like they were ready to draw if I did what they suspected was in my heart.

"You should have fed that investor to the — what was his name? Oh yeah, Parker, Gerald Parker. You should have fed him to the snakes for being such a coward. Can you imagine, a man hiding in the jungle while such a tragedy takes place and not lifting a finger to help?" He shook his head in disgust, making a clicking noise with his tongue.

"How do you know about that?" He'd caught me completely off guard.

The two agents looked at each other in total confusion. It was obvious they had no clue what Taylor was talking about. Hell, they probably didn't even know who he was. All they knew was that the Director himself had called their supervisor with instructions that the man was to be given *anything* he wanted. They were also told that no questions were to be asked. The FBI aren't generally known for their yielding cooperation with anyone outside of their own agency, so they knew Taylor must have some serious stroke somewhere high up the chain of command. When they were told to bring Chance in for a visit, they stepped-and-fetched.

"Chance, I know quite a lot about you. About your past. About your problems. And believe it or not, I also know a great deal about your future." He waggled his finger at Agent Donaldson, and said, "Go get me another cup of coffee." He was putting an explanation mark on who was in charge.

"Who in the hell are you?" I asked for the second time. Frick and Frack might have to kiss this man's ass, but I didn't.

Taylor smiled.

"Do you think this is funny?" I asked. "How about charging me with something or telling me something I don't already know." I was tired, irritated, and way past the end of my rope with these guys and their bullshit.

Taylor was more than pleased with the response. Not backing down an inch under pressure. Just one more of the psychological triggers he looked for in a potential operative.

"Chance, I'd like to give you a very special opportunity. Interested?"

"An opportunity? What, you want me to start selling wonder vitamins and joy juice to all my friends and family? Build a network and get rich? Thanks, but I've already got a job — think I'll pass." I stood up to leave, pitching my cup in the trash.

"Sell vitamins and joy juice," Taylor laughed. "No, I'm talking about killing those little demons that eat away at your insides in the middle of the night. You know, the ones that haunt your dreams, making you ask yourself: Was it my fault? Was there something else I could have done? Why did this happen to me? To Cristina? To my men?"

That stopped me cold.

Taylor pushed himself up from the edge of the desk. He ignored Agent Donaldson's offer of the coffee, letting the man just stand there holding it in his hand.

Donaldson looked at his partner. They didn't have a clue what was going on but got the distinct impression they were about to be dismissed like the errand boys they'd been.

"How about you and I take a little walk," Taylor said, reaching over and patting Chance on the shoulder.

"Sounds good." I felt comfortable with the man and was dying to know what he had in mind for stopping those demons that gnawed away at me during too many sleepless nights. Plus, I really liked the way he'd dismissed the two "feebies".

As we stood outside the office door, waiting for the elevator, Taylor looked back at Agent Donaldson. "You really should put some ice on that jaw. It's starting to look pretty bad." He turned and winked at me.

Not a word was said during the ride down. My mind raced. Taylor was as calm as a man heading to his favorite restaurant.

Once back in the lobby, I looked over at the security guard, still sitting behind his desk. He was holding a half-eaten doughnut with one hand and adjusting the TV antennae with the other. I snapped him a mock salute, and then Taylor and I walked out into the early hours of morning.

"Chance, I'm not going to beat around the bush. I know who was responsible for that slaughter in your camp, and I'm going to give you an opportunity to even the score."

"What do you mean *who* was responsible? It was a mob of pissed-off, drunken villagers. And how in the hell can you give me a shot at getting even? What are you talking about?" The dam had broken, and torrents of hard questions flooded through my mind.

"Take a deep breath," he said. "I know it's tough to soak it all in, but we don't have a lot of time, or the luxury to dance around for months on end to bring you into this deal." He pulled a pack of cigarettes out of his pocket. He shook one loose, offering it to Chance.

"Yeah, why not. Gave them up a while back, but I think I could use one right about now." He flicked open his Zippo and lit mine first, and then fired up his own.

"There was one man behind that attack on your camp." One of his informants heard about Parker's drunken sermon in Chulumani. He said they believed he was masquerading as dredge miner, but was really an operative for the DEA, orchestrating a plan to destroy the local coca fields. That would have brought way too much heat down on their operation, so they gave the order for the attack."

"But we *were* dredge miners," I said, pulling a long drag off my smoke.

"It didn't matter what you were, or who you were. It's what they thought you *might* have been that mattered. Some of those comments Parker made in the *teatro* that night was all it took to make them suspicious, and you know even suspicions can bring a death sentence with those guys." He turned his head and blew a stream of smoke downwind.

"Who put out the order?" I asked.

"We'll get to that in a minute, *if* you want in."

"In what?"

"Justice, my friend. Full scale, balls-to-the-wall, no punches pulled, justice."

"I was reliving it all in my mind. Seeing the bodies of my mutilated friends scattered around camp. The smoldering huts. The stench of violent death. And Cristina, with those lifeless eyes staring into the heavens. I remembered every vivid detail, just like I did in my nightmares, every single night.

"Go on," I said.

Taylor was pleased. Another hurdle passed.

"I want you to eliminate the man who was responsible for the attack."

"How?"

I'll tell you the "how" when the time comes." He reached into his pocket and pulled out an envelope. "There's a ticket for a flight to La Paz that leaves in few days. There's also ten grand in cash to help you catch up on some bills around here before you go. If anyone asks, you can tell them you've decided to go back and try your luck at mining for gold again.

"What about…"

Taylor raised his hand.

"We've got to take this one step at a time, and for now, that's it."

I couldn't completely wrap my mind around all that was happening. My gut was telling me it was the right thing to do, and God knows I'd love the opportunity to deal with the sick son-of-a-bitch responsible for the massacre. I had an airline ticket and a pocket full of more cash than I'd had in a long time, so why not?"

"All right, I'm in," I said.

Taylor nodded, satisfied that he had his man reeled in. "Do you remember the Parque Mirador in La Paz?"

"Yeah, I know the place," I said.

"Meet me there, at midnight on the night you arrive."

I reached out and shook his hand. There were still trainloads of unanswered questions roaring through my mind, but I was focused on the fact that I was going back to Bolivia and might have the opportunity to settle a long overdue debt.

• • •

I arrived in La Paz five days later. A few minutes before midnight I stood in front of the locked gate at the Parque Mirador. It was bitter cold. La Paz sits at an altitude of over twelve-thousand feet — highest capital city in the world. There was a light mist in the air and a stiff breeze that chilled me to the bone. I shivered and pushed my hands deeper into the pockets of my leather jacket.

A *gringo* standing on a dark street in the middle of the night anywhere in Bolivia isn't the safest thing to do. The Beretta 9mm I had snug at the small of my back made me feel more confident. I'd gotten the carry permit when I'd first moved to Bolivia. It had cost me over a thousand dollars in "special processing fees" — aka: bribes, which seemed unreasonably high at the time. Right now, it felt worth every penny.

Just as it did every hour on the hour, my watch chirped with an electronic beep. Midnight on the dot.

"The first thing you've got to do is get rid of that watch," someone said, sneaking up and startling me.

"Jesus, you scared the hell out of me!" I said, easing the grip on my pistol after realizing who it was.

Taylor moved past me and began picking the heavy cast iron lock on the gate. He went about it nonchalantly, like it was something everyone did.

"In the quiet of the night, or the still silence of the jungle, it will give away your position and get you killed. Now, come on, let's go up top and talk."

We walked up the steep steps to the upper level. Even though both of us were in excellent physical condition, we labored on the climb. The altitude was tough on the unaccustomed.

"Beautiful view, isn't it?" Taylor took a seat on a concrete bench and leaned back against the rock wall, motioning for me to sit next to him. He pulled out his smokes, offering me the pack. I waved it off.

"Yeah, it's breathtaking," I said, sarcastically. "But I doubt you dragged me six thousand miles from home to show me the highlights from a travel brochure."

"Alright. You've come this far, so you deserve some answers." He shifted sideways on the cold cement bench so he could look Chance square in the eye. "The man who ordered the raid on your camp is someone every major law enforcement agency in the world has been after for years. But as it is with most of his kind, he has the money and paid-for influence to elude every attempt that's been made to bring him to justice. His crimes are as gruesome as you could ever imagine, but with all the legal red tape and other horse shit the lawyers and politicians can manufacture, he's been bulletproofed. Then, you come along." He pulled the collar of his double-breasted wool pea coat up higher on his neck and flicked a half-smoked cigarette into the darkness, watching the spray of sparks cascade down the hillside. "We have informants in all of his operations, so we heard about the attack on your camp. Unfortunately, it was two days *after*, and too late do anything about it. Once we got the complete report, we found out that you had survived. That's when I started checking you out."

"Why check me out?" It still wasn't clicking for me.

"Because you fit the profile."

"Profile?"

"In a minute," he said. He stood up and stamped his feet, still trying to fend off the cold. "Look, Chance, you're in your late-thirties, good physical condition, and you bailed off into the middle of the Amazon to search for gold. I'd say that marks you as a little out of the ordinary, wouldn't you?"

I nodded, wanting him to continue.

"You were surviving in a country and a culture you knew nothing about. That indicated you were most certainly adaptable." He sat back down. "Your drastic career shift from the suit-and-tie-crowd to a bouncer, and then to chase some *Indiana Jones* adventure down in the Amazon, showed you were definitely ready for some serious changes in life. Am I right so far?"

"Yeah, I'd say you're hitting the nail pretty square on the head. But I still don't..." I got cut off again.

"It truly is tragic what happened, but through it all, you didn't crack. You introverted a bit, but that's to be expected. You held yourself together, and from my perspective, that's what's most telling." He tapped another cigarette out of the pack. He didn't light it but rolled it between his thumb and forefinger. "A while back I was given the green light to eliminate the man who ordered that attack on your camp. It was becoming blatantly clear that it would never get done through conventional channels, so I got the call. One of our biggest challenges has been that the man's intelligence network is just too damned good. I can't use professional operatives without the risk that he'd know they were coming the moment they climbed off the plane."

I was beginning to see where this might be going.

"Then, you come into the picture. You've been around here for a few years and the locals know you. Sure, they gave you the usual cold shoulder in the beginning, just like they do with any foreigner. But they finally accepted you for what you were — a dredge miner and some wild-assed adventurer. And in case you didn't already know it, that's why you weren't killed in the attack."

"What?" That last tidbit got my attention.

"The locals knew you didn't have anything to do with what they suspected Gerald Parker might be involved in, so they let you live.

"Why did they kill Cristina, and my crew?"

"You know how they feel about women down here. They're expendable — a party favor when the time is right." Taylor shook his head in disgust at the truth of his explanation. He'd seen it time and time again in Third World countries around the globe.

"And my crew?"

"Same thing. Expendable. Collateral damage. Just a bunch of villagers who got in the way. Easier to kill them than to recruit them. Simple as that."

Sadly, I knew he was telling the truth. Life was cheap in this part of the world.

"And Parker, he just slithered away in the night like the slimy slug that he is. And even though they didn't kill him, they knew he'd never be back."

"Damn shame about that," I said.

"Chance, you don't have any military or law enforcement background, so no matter how hard they look, they'll never suspect you."

"Suspect me for what?" I was pretty sure I knew what was coming, but I wanted to hear him say the words.

"As the shooter. I want you to take out Ramiro Dueñas.

There it was, right between the eyes, and just like I wanted it. I knew who Dueñas was. He was front page news about something every week. He was either paying for building a new clinic in some impoverished area, donating supplies to underprivileged school kids, or some other bullshit charitable work he used to mask what his life was really about — drugs, violence, and all the evil that went along with it.

"I'm not a killer."

"It's not about being a killer," Taylor said. "The man is a cancer to society and needs to be extracted. We need you to be the surgeon that takes him out. I know you've been a hunter and around guns all your life, so a little time on a secure range we've got set up down here and you'll be up to speed in no time. Plus, I've got everything you need right here in La Paz."

"I don't know," I said, wrestling with my conscience.

"Chance, my gut tells me you're ready to do this." He paused for a moment. "No matter what the liberal factions are preaching back in the States, communism isn't dead in South America. It's alive and well and poses a serious threat to the United States. Even more serious, Islamic radicalism is taking hold down here and building a strong foundation that poses an even greater threat, and not just to the U.S., but to the world. And buddy, if you don't think the drug trade is helping to finance it all, then you've got your head buried in the sand. Men like Ramiro Dueñas have to be dealt with and dealt with now."

Taylor had given his final pitch.

"When would you want me to do it?" I was starting to feel the seed of retribution sprouting up inside me. I wish I could say that all of Taylor's patriotic ramblings had struck a chord, but the truth was, I just wanted to deal with the son-of-a-bitch who'd blown such a devastating hole through the middle of my life. I wanted justice for Cristina.

"So, you're saying you'll do it?" Taylor asked.

"I'm just asking questions," I said.

"That's not how it works. There are no more questions. Either you're in, or you're out. And if you decide you're in — and listen to me very carefully — there is absolutely no turning back."

"Okay, I'm in." I could feel the weight of the swift sword of justice in my hand. I liked the way it felt.

"Outstanding!" Taylor was beyond pleased. "Dueñas has a birthday celebration planned at one of his villas in about six weeks. Before the party, he and a Bolivian army colonel are scheduled to inspect his newest remote field operation. It's not far from the Peruvian border, and in an area where you've prospected for gold before. Your presence around there shouldn't stir up any suspicions. You'll decide how to go in, and how to get out when it's done. Tomorrow morning, a suitcase will be delivered to your hotel. It will come from the airport marked as a piece of luggage that didn't arrive on time with your flight. Tell them you're expecting it, and nobody will even give it a second thought.

"What's in the..."

Taylor held up his hand.

"Inside, you'll find an intel dossier with location coordinates and a held-held GPS unit. Memorize the information and burn the file. You do *not* want to get caught with something like that on you. Understand?"

"Yeah, I got it." I knew I was ass-deep in alligators now. "If something goes wrong, how do I get in touch with you?"

Taylor's face took on a hard, deadly expression. "You don't. If anything goes sideways, or you get caught, you'll be on your own. You'll be an **Outlaw Traveler,** pure and simple. I don't exist, and we never met. And one more thing," he said.

"Oh, this should be good." I managed a half-hearted smile.

"The suitcase you get tomorrow will have another ten thousand dollars in it to offset any expenses you might have down here. When you..."

"I'm not doing this for money," I said, cutting him off.

"When you finish the job and get back to the States, you'll receive a package with a hundred grand in it," he continued. "How you deal with the cash is going to be your problem. Just like me, it never existed. Don't be expecting a 1099 at the end of the year. Understand?"

"I *said...*"

"Yeah, yeah, I know. You're not doing it for the money. But believe me, you'll earn every last cent by the time this is over."

"What about this secure range you were talking about?"

"I'll get word to you in a few days. They'll have your weapon there. Use the range as much as you need. There's a bunkhouse where you can bivouac while you train. You'll be the one who decides when you're ready. I guarantee, you can trust anybody that's there. Use them. Pick their brains. Take advantage of their expertise. They're the best in the business. And Chance, you need to understand, those men operate on the Three Monkey Principle: See no evil. Hear no evil. And tell nobody a damn thing when it's over. They won't ask any questions about why you're there, and they won't want to know what you're planning when you leave. And after you're gone, as far as they'll be concerned, you never existed."

He offered me another cigarette. I took it this time.

Taylor stood up, stamped his feet, and then reached down and shook Chance's hand. "Good luck," he said, and quietly walked off into the night.

I stayed seated on the hard stone bench, chilled to the bone, wondering what in the hell I was getting myself into now.

CHAPTER 12

THE telephone rang, jolting him out of a deep sleep like a bucket of ice water in the face. He reached over the warm bundle of joy that was his wife, buried deep under a heavy layer of blankets and fumbled the receiver up to his ear.

"Hello." His voice was thick with sleep.

"Your interest payments are due in less than a week, and a little birdie tells me you might not have the dough." The man's voice was rough and full of menace — a predator roaming the darkness.

"Uh, yeah, I know. Things have been a tough lately. I might need a little more time, but you know I'm good for it."

"Hey, skid-mark! You're out of time and we're out of patience," threatened the night caller. "And how's that sweet little wife of yours? I always wondered what a juicy little mama like that was doing with a loser like you. I bet I could put a *real* smile on her face." He'd never mentioned his wife like that before. "You're a lucky man, but your luck is about to run out if you don't get us our fucking money."

"Surely we can work something out. I'm doing everything I can. You know I've always paid in the past." A knot tightened in the pit of his gut. There was frost on the windows but sweat trickled down his face.

The line went dead.

He reached over his sleeping wife and dropped the phone onto the nightstand, and then sank back into the warm spot on his side of the bed. A violent shiver wracked his body as he pulled the blanket snug under his chin. It didn't help. It wasn't the cold that had him. It was fear.

His wife stirred and snuggled up against him, forming herself to the contours of his body like people do who've shared the same bed for many years — comfortable and uninhibited. She laid her arm across his chest.

"Who was that on the phone?" she mumbled, still half asleep.

"Nobody, honey. Just go back to sleep." He slid his hand under the covers and rubbed it along the curve of her backside. She purred deep in her chest like a cat. He knew she loved it, and now he wished he'd done it for her more often. He swung his legs over the side of the bed and sat up, startling when his bare feet hit the cold tile floor. "What am I going to do? What in the hell am I going to do?" He cradled his head in both hands and moaned.

Up to this point he had led a fairly sheltered life. He'd only known real fear once, and that incident had driven him into a thumb-sucking fetal position, curled up on the ground while mayhem wreaked havoc just a few yards away. He still remembered the screaming, the roaring blaze of burning huts, and hiding like a coward in the jungle while others died.

Now, he had no place to hide. His pursuers knew where he was and how to hurt him the most. He stood naked before the whip.

Gerald Parker was not a strong man.

CHAPTER 13

HALFWAY across the country, the man who'd called Gerald Parker was on the phone again. This time the conversation took on a much different tone.

"Yes, sir. I rattled his cage real good," he said. "And when I mentioned how sweet I thought his old lady was, he sounded like he was pissing all over himself."

"That's good, Frank. And listen, even though I know I asked you to let me know as soon as you made contact, next time, let's try and be a little more considerate with what time you call. Okay?"

"Oh, yes sir. Sorry about that."

J. Edward killed the connection.

Frank Jacobson was a man who had been referred to as being as big as the side of a barn since he was fourteen years old. And in that same West Texas vernacular he'd grown up around, he'd also been described as being as dumb as a stump. Things didn't change much as he grew older, except that his voracious appetite insured he continued to get even larger, and coincidentally, dumber at about the same rate.

Jacobson reached over and slapped his meaty hand hard against the exposed butt of the woman lying next to him. It made a sharp crack and she jumped up off the bed.

"Shit, Frank! What the hell was that for?" She was stark naked, rubbing the giant red welt on her right butt cheek.

"Get the hell out of here," he ordered. "I've got some important stuff to think about and you're distracting me."

She picked up a half-smoked joint from an ashtray on top of the television and fired it up. She sucked in a deep drag, held it in her lungs for a few seconds, and then coughed out the acrid smoke. "You're an ass, Frank," she sputtered.

"Yeah, and you're a whore!" He wadded up five crisp one-hundred-dollar bills and threw them at her. "There! Take your money and shuffle the hell out of here before you ruin my good mood."

She picked up three of the bills that landed at her feet but had to get down flat on her stomach and root around under the bed to find the other two. She stormed into the bathroom and slammed the door shut behind her.

Frank Jacobson might very well be a pain in the ass, but he paid well, and he didn't knock her around too much. There was something to be said for that. Besides, putting up with guys like him went along with the job.

Jacobson was naked and sprawled out on the bed. He took the remote and began flipping through the channels, hoping he might get lucky and catch a sleazy movie.

"Ain't life great?" he hollered at the bathroom door, not knowing if she could hear him over the noise of the shower.

She heard but ignored him. She was paid and off the clock.

Jacobson laced his fingers behind his head. He crossed one heavy leg over the other and squirmed around, trying to find a comfortable position. He finally hit on a station where two naked bodies writhed together in the back seat of a car — his idea of educational television.

Frank Jacobson was indeed a happy man. He was staying in a posh boutique hotel in the Coconut Grove section of Miami with a pocket full of cash and a good-looking hooker in his bathroom. *What else could a man want out of life?* he thought. Going to work for J. Edward Adams III had been the best break he'd ever gotten, and he planned on milking it for all it was worth.

"Who would have ever thought that a washed-up semi-pro football player would end up a big-time corporate executive?" he said to the closed bathroom door. The shower had stopped so he was sure that she could hear him now.

"Yeah, Frank, you're a real hot-shot executive — an executive thug," she said, sarcastically. She cracked open the door and a cloud of steam rolled out into the room.

"Better than sucking dick for a living!" he shot back.

"Not by much," she added.

"Whatever." He thought about it for a second. "Next time, I'll call someone else!"

"Good!" She kicked the door closed with her heel.

Jacobson went back to watching the movie. He hoped it wouldn't be long before Mr. Adams cut him loose on Gerald Parker. Besides, he really did have a little thing for the man's wife. It made him smile to think about it.

CHAPTER 14

I **WALKED** out of the Hotel Copacabana a little after eleven o'clock. At a brisk pace it would only take me about thirty minutes to get to the Parque Mirador. I planned on taking my time and decided going on foot would attract less attention than having a cab drop me off at the entrance to a closed park in the middle of the night. Besides, a nice stroll would give me an opportunity to think things through a little.

Even at this late hour, the sidewalks around the hotel were crowded with street vendors selling everything from soft drinks and disposable razors to hand-woven alpaca sweaters. Capitalism at its finest.

The ever-present beggars sat huddled in doorways, bobbing open palms in hope of a few coins. I dropped some change into a tin can in front of a blind woman who was banging a broken tambourine and singing. I wasn't sure which was worse, the banging or her caterwauling, but I had to give her credit for trying.

I turned the corner onto a dark street. The activity on the *prado* disappeared behind me. There were no streetlights or vendors, just one long deserted street after another that would lead me to the park, and to my meeting with Don Taylor.

I flipped up the collar of my jacket, balled my fists deep into my pockets, and picked up the pace, walking head-on into the bitter wind. I could feel the cold metal of the 9mm pressed at the small of my back. It gave me the same comfort that it always did.

I could hear the low rumble of a car pulling up behind me and thought it odd that it wasn't moving fast enough to go past. That same intuition that has kept me alive all these years started kicking in. The hair stood stiff on the back of my neck and I felt that familiar, eerie twinge in the pit of my stomach. Something wasn't right. I never ignored my gut instincts and didn't think this was a good time to start.

I heard gravel crunching as the car's tires gripped the street and lurched forward. Glancing back over my shoulder, I could see what looked like the barrel of a cut-down shotgun sticking out from the backseat window, and instantly realized what was coming. The driver stomped on the accelerator and sped forward, pulling parallel to my position. Just as the shotgun roared, I fell hard to a shoulder roll on the sidewalk. Glass exploded form a storefront window and rained down on me as I sprang up, drawn pistol in hand.

A second blast erupted from the speeding car, but it was too far ahead for the shooter to be accurate. I squatted low and fired off several quick shots. I couldn't see much in the darkness but heard at least two of my rounds hammer into the vehicle and one shatter their rear window. I knew I missed the driver because the car fishtailed wildly around the corner and disappeared.

Pumped full of combat adrenaline, my mind slammed into gear and raced through the choices of what I needed to do next. The first thing was to try and stay calm. The next was to get the hell out of there. Even on a deserted street with no witnesses, someone was bound to have heard the shooting and called the police.

I double-timed it around the same corner my attackers had taken, my weapon held ready in front of me. Then, I sprinted down a side street and back toward the *prado*. Once on the crowded thoroughfare, I hailed a taxi. I slipped the pistol into my coat pocket and made a mental note that I only had a few rounds left in the magazine. I kept a firm grip on the weapon, just in case.

I glanced at my watch. 11:20 p.m. The action in the street made it seem like I'd left the hotel hours ago, when in reality, it had only been about twenty minutes. It's odd how adrenaline and fear warps time. Now, I just needed to figure out who in the hell wanted me dead.

CHAPTER 15

ALAN Breckenridge sat in the VIP suite on the upper level of the Club Amazonas. The music downstairs was so loud and heavy with bass that it vibrated the floor. Cocaine was piled up like little sugar mountains on the table in front of him. There were about twenty people in the room. Most of them were extremely beautiful young women in various stages of undress. Some were completely naked. All of them were either drunk, stoned, or a combination of both. The ones still coherent enough gave him varying degrees of come-hither looks, doing exactly what they'd been paid to do — entertain and be available. This wasn't Breckenridge's idea of the ideal environment considering the serious nature of their business, but he'd been waiting for two days, and this was the only time and place Colonel Zoto would agree to meet.

The colonel was molded into a faux leather sofa pushed up against the wall across from Breckenridge. A nude, mocha-skinned girl was passed out, lying face down in his lap. Another equally lovely young lady with lost, vacant eyes, was down on her knees, snorting cocaine through a glass tube she had buried in a pile of powder in front of her.

Colonel Zoto grabbed a handful of the girl's hair in his lap and slung her tiny body to the side like a discarded rag doll. He kicked the girl in front of him so hard she sprawled flat across the table, scattering a cloud of white powder all over the front of Breckenridge's dark suit. "Now, what is it you are so anxious to talk to me about?" he asked.

"Colonel, it's about our shipment," Breckenridge said. He leaned across the table, glancing at the others around the room. "We need to know when we can expect delivery."

"*El gringito* here wants to know when they'll get their drugs!" Zoto roared in laughter. That got everyone's attention — at least the few still sober enough to know what was going on.

The room fell deadly silent, and then everyone burst into howls of laughter, pointing at Breckenridge and mocking him. He'd tried to be discreet, but now it was obvious that everyone there knew the details of his involvement.

"Let me tell you something, *chico*," Zoto said, in a threatening tone. "It is nothing but pure luck that I didn't get my head blown off just like Ramiro Dueñas did. *Mireda!* I was standing right next to him when he got hit!" He reached across the table and seized Breckenridge by the knot of his tie, jerking him within inches of his face. Breckenridge could smell the odor of cheap cigars, whiskey, and who knows what else on the man's breath. "We were this close — this fucking close!" He opened his eyes wide, and in a menacing whisper, said, "You'll get your drugs when I find out what the hell is going on, and not one second sooner." He shoved Breckenridge violently back across the table.

Breckenridge settled into his chair and stared at the man for a moment, considering his options. "With all due respect, my employer advanced a ten-million-dollar deposit. I think he deserves to know a little more than that."

Zoto licked the top half of his right index finger and plunged it deep into one of the white mounds on the table, and then rubbed it across his upper gums, smacking his lips. "*Escúchame, pendejo.* When I am certain all is secure, *then* we will move forward."

Breckenridge didn't respond. He just sat and waited, hoping Colonel Zoto would elaborate more, and dumbfounded that he was so unaffected by the amount of cocaine he'd just ingested.

"Now, if that isn't satisfactory, you can tell your *jefe* he can come down here and ask me for a refund himself." He roared another menacing laugh.

Breckenridge nodded slowly.

Colonel Zoto leaned across the table, and in a voice so low that Breckenridge had to strain to hear him, said, "In other words, you little *maricòn*, remember where you are and who you are dealing with."

"I'll remember that, colonel, and thank you for your time." Breckenridge stood up to leave, knowing full well that he'd pushed matters as far as he could. He attempted to brush the white powder off his slacks. He knew J. Edward was not going to be pleased with the colonel's attitude or his explanation, but he could better deal with a pissed-off boss, than with what Zoto would surely do to him if he pressed things any further.

Live to fight another day. The old adage popped into Breckenridge's mind. It seemed like damn good advice.

CHAPTER 16

STOOD in front of the iron gate at Parque Mirador. It was two minutes before midnight, and I knew that Taylor would be here soon. Hopefully, he'd have some answers.

"At least your watch didn't give you away this time."

"Damnit! Why do you do that?" Even though I'd been watching for him, he still snuck up on me.

"Because it amuses me," he said. "What's got you so jumpy?"

"Oh, I don't know. Someone just tried to blow my fucking head off with a shotgun."

Taylor remained calm. "In that case, let's change things up a little. I've got a car parked about a block from here. It'll be a lot safer than sitting out in the open until we know what's going on."

"Change things up a little? That's all you've got to say?"

Taylor shrugged his shoulders. Steady as Gibraltar.

"In the car. Then we'll talk," he said.

It took about three minutes to walk to the car, the silence like irritating needles stabbing at my curiosity.

"Here she is." He nodded toward a 1974 Plymouth Duster. It was faded red with a ratty-looking white vinyl top and black-wall tires. No hubcaps.

"What a piece of junk," I mumbled.

"She might not look like much, but she runs like a bat out of hell."

I walked around to the other side of the old sled and pulled open the passenger door. It groaned like it hadn't seen a can of oil in years. When I slammed it shut, the whole car rattled.

"Nice," I said.

Taylor buckled himself in and cranked over the engine. The motor jumped to life and I felt like I was sitting on a jet turbine, ready to scream out of the gate.

"Better buckle up," he said, dropping the selector into drive and tapping the accelerator. The car squealed away from the curb and he quickly pulled her under control, glancing over at me and grinning.

No more snide remarks about the car.

"It belongs to a buddy of mine who does some work down here. Looks like a pile of junk so nobody notices it, but when you need to get up and go, she's a jewel."

We flowed into traffic and headed downtown. It was uncontrolled gridlock at its finest. As the crow flies, it wasn't very far back to the hotel, but with traffic as it was, it would have been quicker to have just walked. On the upside, we'd have plenty of time to talk.

"Now, tell me what happened," Taylor said.

I tried to roll down the window to let in some fresh air. The glass got about halfway down before the handle twisted off in my hand. I gave it a brief look and tossed it into the back seat. Then, I told him about the attack.

Taylor listened intently, mentally chewing and digesting every detail, deciding what adjustments needed to be made. In his world, things seldom went as planned.

Adjust and adapt. That was the name of the game. "How" wasn't the most important part of the puzzle. Getting the job done was all that mattered.

CHAPTER 17

I T was just after midnight and Breckenridge hated to call J. Edward this late, but he knew he'd fly into one of his tirades if he didn't contact him as soon as he had any news. He was probably going to blow a mental gasket either way, so he might as well get it over with. He sat in his dark hotel room, listening to the endless clicks on the line as the call connected, waiting on the unpleasant and the inevitable.

"Residence of Mr. J. Edward Adams III," answered a distinguished voice in a thick British accent.

"This is Alan Breckenridge. I need to speak with Mr. Adams."

"Sir, Mr. Adams is not available at this late hour. Perhaps you should try and call back tomorrow."

"Just get him on the phone, *Jeeves*." He knew the man was J. Edward's butler, and figured the sarcastic jab would get the point of his irritation across more quickly.

Silence. Breckenridge wasn't sure if the man had gone to get J. Edward, or if he'd hung up. Maybe the "Jeeves" jab wasn't such a good idea after all.

An irritated voice finally came on the line.

"Mr. Breckenridge, I hope you have called to inform me that our little situation has been resolved. Otherwise, I am certain you would not have disturbed me at such an unreasonable hour." As always, J.

Edward prefaced the conversation in such a way that no matter what Breckenridge said, it would be wrong. If it was bad news, he'd be pissed-off about that. And if it was good news, he'd still be pissed-off because he was calling so late.

"Well, no sir. Actually, things are still a little uncertain."

Is our shipment going to be delivered, or not?" J. Edward's voice cracked with anger.

"I met with our contact and he said there were still some problems that needed to be worked out. Hopefully, it won't be much longer." He tried to sprinkle a little water of hope onto the fire. It certainly wasn't hope that he'd gotten from Colonel Zoto, but there was no way in hell that he'd tell J. Edward what the man had really said.

"Hopefully?" Is that it? Goddamnit! I knew I should have handled this myself!" J. Edward slammed down the receiver. He couldn't stand it any longer and completely lost his refined demeanor. He swung his walking stick like a baseball bat, knocking the telephone across the room. It slammed into a small antique lamp. The lamp smashed against the wall and glass scattered across the floor. "Clean it up!" he barked at the butler, storming past him and out of the room.

Breckenridge sat on the edge of the bed. He was mentally beaten and frustrated beyond measure. He stared at the buzzing receiver for a moment, and then gently placed it back on the bedside table. He knew he'd be able to catch a flight in about five hours and be back in Oklahoma City tomorrow night. He'd wait and call Lisa when he changed planes in Miami. Without a doubt, she was the one shining star in his dismal life. Then, he'd deal with J. Edward, the devil himself, always rattling skeletons from the past and reminding him of secrets he would never allow to be buried and forgotten.

CHAPTER 18

STARED at Taylor across the front seat of the old Plymouth, distracted by a ragged piece of duct tape that only half covered a hole in the headrest behind him. I'd given him the blow-by-blow details of what happened, and then we tried to come up with anyone that might want me dead.

"We've got a leak," Taylor opined. "A weak link in the chain somewhere, but I'll be damned if I can think of where it might be."

"Is that supposed to give me the warm fuzzier of confidence?" I asked.

"We'll have to be a little more careful from here on out."

"What's this *we* stuff? Seems like the only ass on the line here is mine."

Taylor smiled. He knew this latest incident was like a wide span between two rooftops. Chance had two choices. He could take the risk and leap for the other side, or he could turn back. He wouldn't think any less of him if he turned back. Most men would.

"So, what's it going to be? Move forward, or call it quits?"

"Quit? I didn't say anything about quitting. I just want to know what the hell the new plan is," I said.

One more validation that his initial judgment about Chance had been right. He was one of those rare individuals who had the heart and the mental steel this kind of work demanded.

"Just carry on and I'll take care of the problem," Taylor said.

"Speaking of which, you still haven't told me what you wanted me here for in the first place. We're talking about quitting and moving forward and all that, and I don't even know what the plan was to begin with. I'm sure you didn't drag me all the way over here just to pat me on the back for what happened to Ramiro Dueñas. You don't remind me of the hugs and roses type of guy."

"Yeah, you did do a hell of a job getting Dueñas handled. So good in fact, that I've got another assignment for you." This time, Taylor didn't even ask Chance if he was interested.

"Don't you think one was enough? I told you before, this isn't my line of work. I settled the score with that piece of human garbage that was responsible for ruining my life. I've got no more axes to grind."

"Ramiro Dueñas was just one rung on a long ladder of misery. The workings of the main shit-machine haven't skipped a beat since you took him off the count. We know we'll never be able to put them completely out of business, but we've got to try and slow their train down as much as we can while we've got the chance. No pun intended."

"What have you got in mind?"

Taylor breathed a sigh of satisfaction. "Now, that Dueñas is out of the picture, someone new has taken the reins, and our intel indicates they're getting ready to put some major weight into the pipeline.

"And?"

"Do you remember Colonel Zoto?"

"You have *got* to be kidding me! I could have popped that guy when I took out Dueñas."

"Actually, I was surprised you didn't?

"I told you. I'm not a killer," I bristled. "You hooked me into taking care of Dueñas because I had a debt to settle. Colonel Zoto wasn't my business."

Taylor liked what he was hearing. Chance wasn't just some reckless trigger-jockey. He'd given him an assignment with a specific target and a reason to carry out the job, and that's exactly what he'd done. No more. No less.

Taylor stopped at a jammed-up intersection. He turned in his seat and looked directly at Chance. "Colonel Zoto picked put the business Dueñas left behind, and we need him to point us to this new player in the States."

"Makes sense, but how do you want me to handle it," I asked.

"Give me a few days and I'll get the details worked out. This new little wrinkle has changed things a bit, but not that much."

"And in the meantime?"

"Lay low and get some rest. You're going to need it."

"Yeah, I can just imagine." I managed a little laugh.

"And change hotels. They took a crack at you tonight which means they knew where you were staying. Might be a good idea to get lost in the crowd for a few days."

"Sure thing," I said. "A six-foot, blonde-haired *gringo* in La Paz, Bolivia. Hiding in the crowd will be a snap."

"Alright, smart-ass. You know what I mean."

Taylor pulled the Plymouth up to the curb in the front of the hotel. I got out of the car.

"Chance!" Taylor hollered.

I walked around the front and leaned down to the driver's side window. "Yeah?"

"Watch your back." He stomped on the gas, squealing his tires and zipping back into the flow of traffic.

I walked up toward the hotel entrance, reaching into the pocket of my jacket and gripping the pistol. The weight felt good in my hand. I made a mental note that I needed to put in a full clip.

CHAPTER 19

GERALD Parker sat in his small executive suite office. It was one of twelve similar spaces in a cluster that shared a common receptionist, a break area, and a conference room. It was in a downtown high-rise, so he still had the outward appearance of great success, even if his career was caving in around his neck.

Parker leaned back in his fake leather swivel chair, staring at the ceiling. He wasn't sure how he'd let things get this far out of hand. He'd started out as a small-time contractor and built his business from the ground up into a thriving enterprise that employed over three hundred people. Nowhere close to the Fortune 500, but certainly nothing to be ashamed of. At least his wife and kids seemed proud of him. He wondered why that couldn't have been enough. Why had he let his ambitions take over his better judgment and cause his life to spiral down the toilet?

He had always paid his bank notes on time, which was a rare thing for anyone in the real estate development business when he started out. The banks had taken notice and valued his accomplishments. They had always seemed willing to work with him in any way they could, but they had limits. Lending limits. That was the excuse they used when the economy started tanking.

Sure, things had taken a little dip, but he knew what he was doing. If they'd just give him a little more time, he was certain he could work his way out of this recession. But they wouldn't budge. The keys to the candy store were gone.

Parker's financial reserves were running dry, and his friendly bankers had turned into rabid wolves, clawing at his front door. He'd gotten so desperate that he scraped together what little cash he could to invest in a wild-assed South American gold mining project, hoping to hit the mother lode quick enough to pull himself out of his ruinous financial pit. At least that's what the slick promoter had promised. When he went down to take a firsthand look at the operation, it turned out to be the biggest disaster of his life, leaving him curled up half naked in a thumb-sucking fetal position on the jungle floor.

Then, it happened. A miracle. A saving hand of salvation swept down out of nowhere and scooped him out of his misery. Frontier Financial Corporation. One of their business development executives had called and said he wanted to meet to discuss consolidating his debts and extending him a new line of credit. Parker never even questioned why. He just grabbed on with both greedy hands. They'd explained that Frontier Financial invested in valuable real estate holdings suffering from the downswing in the economy, and with his record, they were confident he was just the man to pull it all together. The interest rates were unusually high, but like they kept telling him, he was the man that could make it happen.

Like many self-made men, Gerald Parker had no shortage of confidence. Just a little time and little cash and he knew he could make it work.

But things didn't get better. They got progressively worse. Interest compounded upon interest and late payments began stacking up. Parker pleaded for one extension after another, and they'd always been granted — until now.

Frank Jacobson, the friendly business development representative who had contacted Parker initially and stroked his ego until it became a devastating hard-on of irresponsibility, was calling in the middle of the night and demanding money. And if that wasn't bad enough, now he was making veiled threats toward his wife. He should have known from the very beginning that something wasn't right about that man. He didn't seem like any business executive he'd ever known. But he said he had the authority to loan him money, and loan him money he did — truckloads of it.

Now, it was all coming back to haunt him. He could stand to lose the business, but his family, that was something he couldn't allow to be put at risk because of his own stupidity and cowardice.

For the first time in a long time, Gerald Parker sucked it up and summoned what little courage he could and called for help. He was feeling better about himself already. Maybe he had a little backbone left after all.

CHAPTER 20

LISA Dalton was deceptively strong considering her petite frame, but she was certainly no match for the mountainous mass of manhood standing at her front door.

Lisa and Alan shared a condo in an upscale community that had a manned guardhouse at the front gate twenty-four hours a day. The rent-a-cop had called to let her know someone from Alan's office was there with a delivery. She never even thought twice about telling the guard to let him through and didn't give a second thought to opening the front door when he rang the bell.

"Mrs. Breckenridge, I have some paperwork your husband asked to have sent over. I need you to sign for it, please."

Even though she wasn't officially Mrs. Breckenridge, she loved it when people made that assumption, and saw no reason to correct the courier now.

"Certainly." She released the latch on the glass door, pushing it open and reaching for the clipboard.

That was all the opening Frank Jacobson needed. He launched his massive bulk through the door and violently knocked her against the wall. He reached down and enveloped her throat with his hand, snatching her up to the tips of her toes. Now, even if she could scream, she was too terrified to do so.

"I'm here to talk to you about Alan. I've got no interest in hurting you," he said in a calm voice. "Just keep your mouth shut and everything will be fine. But give me a reason, any reason at all, and I might change my mind and teach you a few things I bet your boyfriend never showed you." He licked his lips in a nasty way, making sure she knew the kinds of things he had in mind.

Lisa's eyes were as big as saucers and filled with fear. Jacobson's fingers gripped her neck so tight that she couldn't even nod, so she blinked so he'd know that she understood.

She felt his grip loosen and her heels dropped to the floor. She could breathe again. Lisa rubbed her hands to the welts rising on her neck. She had always heard that it was best to try and stay calm in situations like this. No need to anger her attacker any more than necessary. At least he didn't seem like he planned on hurting her any further. But just in case, she scanned the room, looking for anything she might be able to use as a weapon if things took a turn for the worse.

"May I sit down, please?" she asked.

"Sure, doll, that's fine. But how about grabbing me a beer first? You got some beer around here, don't you?"

Lisa couldn't believe the nerve of this guy. "There's some in the refrigerator below the wet bar — over there." She pointed across the room.

"Lazy-ass women," Jacobson mumbled, blowing out a short breath of disgust. He walked over and grabbed a bottle of beer.

Lisa thought briefly about trying to escape. Maybe she could open the front door and get out before he could get to her. Maybe she could grab a fireplace tool and take a good whack at him. But better judgment prevailed, and she settled into one of the floral-patterned straight-backed chairs. She thought about how much Alan hated the pastel-colored fabric. "Sissy-looking." That's what he'd said when they bought it. But he knew it was what she wanted, so that's what they gotten.

Jacobson didn't see an opener handy, and the bottle didn't have a twist-off cap, so he hammered the top off on the edge of the bar. A chip of ebony marble shot across the room.

"You are a pretty little thing, aren't you? Bet you and me could have us some real fun. Whatcha' think? Want to mess around?" Jacobson took a swig of the ice-cold beer, and then wiped his mouth on his forearm.

Lisa said nothing. Her stomach twisted in knots of terror.

"Relax, I'm just jerkin' your chain," he said, letting out a rumbling burp.

His instructions had been very clear. Do...not...hurt...the... woman. They'd said it just like that, like he was stupid or something. Even though he hadn't appreciated the implications, he'd taken his orders to heart

"We need to talk about Alan."

"Oh, my God! What have you done to him?" Lisa felt a cold shiver run up her spine. "Is he okay?" Her voice quivered and she trembled with fear. Tears welled up in her eyes.

"Yeah, yeah, he's fine. But he has been a *very* bad boy," Jacobson said, reaching over and grabbing the file he'd brought with him. He tossed it into Lisa's lap.

"What's this?" She was afraid to open it.

"Come on, honey, take a peek. It won't bite." He took another swig of beer.

Lisa unwound the clasp and dumped the contents out onto the coffee table. She gave everything a cursory look at first, and then studied each document more carefully. It was gruesome eight-by-ten black and white crime scene photos, mixed in with page after page of typewritten detail. The more she studied the documents, the more she realized they were about Alan. The man she loved. The man she shared her life with. The man she wanted to marry. The man she *thought* she knew.

All of Alan Breckenridge's ugly skeletons were scattered out before her. All the things he'd never wanted her to know. All his deepest, darkest secrets, in vivid, morbid detail. Tears streamed down her face and sobs wracked her body. She couldn't believe what she was seeing.

"Okie-dokie," Jacobson said. "Looks like my job here is done. Maybe I'll see you again sometime. Still bet we could have us some fun."

He winked at her, and then pitched the empty beer bottle on the rug on his way out the door.

Lisa didn't even look up.

CHAPTER 21

J. EDWARD was more relaxed this evening than he'd been in quite some time. Sure, there had been problems that had thrown a kink in his plans, but things were finally starting to look up. He'd chided himself for not personally taking care of the situation from the very beginning. At least now he knew that when it was all finally over, the chaff will have been sifted from the wheat of his organization.

The visitor seated in his study wasn't quite as at ease. He didn't like being summoned to the man's home. Even the remote possibility that someone might see him there was an enormous risk.

"Mr. Adams, I'm glad the information I gave you was useful, but really, meeting like this isn't a good idea — not for either of us."

"Relax," J. Edward said. "I am well aware of the risk, but I thought it better to thank you personally for all you've done, and to express my gratitude more properly." He eased himself into a sturdy straight-back chair at his desk.

"There's no need for anything else, Mr. Adams. You've already been more than generous." He nervously ran his finger along the inside of his collar.

J. Edward took two banded stacks of hundred-dollar bills and slid them over in front of his visitor. Twenty-thousand dollars.

The man picked up the cash, putting one bundle into each of his inside suit coat pockets. It made uncomfortable and noticeable bulges.

"There, now isn't that better?" J. Edward smiled.

"Thank you, sir."

"I am sure I will need your help again, and I am assuming it will be alright to give you a call when I do."

"Yes, sir, you may." The man knew it would be better to end his dealings with J. Edward altogether, but he also knew that wasn't an option at this point.

"Good, then I will be in touch," J. Edward said, pushing himself up from behind the desk.

The man stood and offered his hand. J. Edward ignored the gesture. He made it a practice not to shake hands with anyone he considered beneath him, so he just left the man standing there, feeling awkward.

Agent Donaldson pulled back his hand. *Asshole*, he thought, and walked out of the room, twenty-thousand dollars richer. He wondered if the money was worth the part of himself that he was selling.

CHAPTER 22

I SAT on the edge of the bed, my weight causing the opposite corner of the cheap mattress to pop up in the air. The sheets weren't fitted so they pulled to the center.

The room was pitiful. There was a small wooden table, but no chair. The only bathroom was at the end of the hall and serviced the entire floor. The television downstairs in the lobby only had three black and white channels. The choices tonight were soccer, *novelas*, or reruns of *Los Simpsons* dubbed in Spanish. I didn't think *Homero Simpson* would tickle my funny bone tonight.

Don Taylor suggested that I get lost in the city for a few days. This should do it. I crossed one leg over the other, and then crossed them back again. There wasn't a comfortable position to be had and I was bored out of my mind.

The Hotel Santa Isabela was in the San Fernando District of La Paz. To say the least, the area wasn't much to write home about. The steep streets were crowded with sidewalk shops that were tended by indigenous Indian women wearing brown bowler hats and huge colorful skirts — traditional *cholita* attire. And in this neighborhood, they trucked in loads of trash after midnight, dumping it in the middle of the street and burning it.

At least nobody knew I was here. Or so I thought.

Three sharp knocks rattled the flimsy wooden door. I stood up and the floor creaked loudly. So much for pretending nobody was home. Of course, there wasn't a peephole, so I picked up the Beretta and worked back the action, making sure there was a round in the chamber. I flattened myself against the wall.

"*Si?*" I said gruffly.

"Chance, it's me. Let me in."

It was Taylor. I slid back the lock and opened the door.

"Nice to see you, too," he said, stepping into the room and taking immediate notice of the pistol. "You think you might ease the hammer down on that thing and point it somewhere else?"

I thumbed down the hammer and laid it on the table.

Taylor made a quick appraisal of the room. A sly grin crept across his face. "Nice digs. Sort of goes along with the old Plymouth."

"Cute," I said. "What did you find out?" I was sick of being cooped up, and if I was going to do this thing, I wanted to get on with it.

Taylor looked around for a chair, finally sitting on the edge of the bed. The far end of the mattress popped up.

"Jesus, Chance, is this the best you could do?"

"Yeah, yeah, I know." I leaned back against the edge of the table.

"I couldn't find the leak," he said, firing up his customary smoke. "To say the least, my chain of command is pretty short. There are only a handful of people that even know I exist, much less what I'm doing. And there's only one man who knows you're working for me, and he's as solid as they come. In other words, blank wall." He looked around and didn't see an ashtray or a trashcan, so he flicked his ashes on the scarred wooden floor, doubting it would mar the decor.

"Is that supposed to make me feel better?" I asked.

"I think we should move forward. You've just got to watch your back," he said.

"Great plan," I mumbled.

"Whoever tried to take you out could have done it for some other reason than what we've got going on now. Believe it or not, there are groups down here who aren't huge fans of the old red-white-and-blue, and buddy, you're about as "apple pie" as they come."

I didn't respond.

"The truth — it could have been a result of the job you did on Ramiro Dueñas. Maybe someone figured out you were the one that took him out. We might as well face the facts — it is a possibility."

"In other words, I've been ass-deep in alligators all along, only now you're telling me I've got a ten-pound sack of bloody pork chops hanging off my belt?"

"Could be." He was being brutally honest.

I chewed on my bottom lip, thinking things through. "Since we're already this far out in the river, it's about as easy to swim on over to the other side as it is to turn back now."

Don Taylor had waited a long time to find a man with Chance's mettle. He just hoped he wouldn't lose him on his second assignment.

CHAPTER 23

FRANK Jacobson admired the extravagant surroundings in the main offices of Frontier Financial Corporation. Since he was a field agent, he usually worked out of his apartment, but on those rare occasions he was invited to the office he played it for all it was worth.

Sitting next to him on the leather sofa was one of his regular rent-a-dates. She was decked out in a purple sequined mini skirt and black leather boots that rose just above the tops of her knees. Pink fishnet stockings covered the distance between her boots and where her skirt hit high up on her thighs. She sported a tight lavender sweater that looked at least two sizes too small, and most of her silicone "ta-tas", as Jacobson liked to call them, spilled out over her plunging neckline. Her makeup was just as gaudy and distracting. Jacobson had told her to dress up for the occasion. This was what she'd come up with.

The women that worked in the office tried to ignore her, rolling their eyes each time she popped her gum. They secretly thought that if there was a brass pole in the center of the room, she'd be swinging on it.

The ornate French doors to the main office swung open and Adele Carter walked out into the lobby.

"Mr. Jacobson, you may go in now."

"Come on, cutie, let's go!" Jacobson swelled with pride. He unwound his massive six-foot-six frame from the couch, and then reached down and grabbed his companion's hand, pulling her up to his side.

Adele Carter frowned. "Frank, I really do think it would be best if you went in alone."

"Alone? Oh, hell no!" he said. "I want to introduce Lacey to Mr. Adams." He bulled past the reception desk with his companion in tow. Her six-inch spike heels tap-tap-tapped across the polished parquet floor.

"Excuse me, *granny*," Lacy snapped. She took a thick wad of gum out of her mouth and stuck it on the wall by the door as she pushed by.

J. Edward's eyebrows arched at the sight of Jacobson and his guest. "Frank, I would prefer that we discussed our business in private."

"Oh, I know," Jacobson said. "But we're thinking about getting married and I wanted Lacy to meet my boss."

J. Edward frowned, and then forced a smile. "Very well. It is nice to meet you, Miss Lacey. Now, would you please excuse us?"

Lacey blushed.

Jacobson beamed. "Okay, baby. Go sit your cute little ass on the couch and I'll be done in a minute. Then, we'll go to the Sizzler for supper." He swatted her on the butt as she turned to leave. She let out a ridiculous schoolgirl giggle.

After she was gone, J. Edward gave Jacobson a stern, fatherly look of disapproval. He'd learned a long time ago that dealing with illiterate behemoths like him demanded a special approach.

"Hell, I'm not really going to marry her," Jacobson said. "I just thought she might throw me a "freebie" if I said that."

That reaffirmed J. Edward's notion that the man was a complete moron. But he did what he was told without asking questions, so he tolerated him. At least for the time being.

"I'm glad if I have helped you in any way with your — with your negotiations." J. Edward couldn't bring himself to use the word "freebie".

"Thanks, boss," Jacobson said. "And I really am taking her to the Sizzler."

"How did your meeting go with Breckenridge's fiancée?" J. Edward asked, steering the conversation back to the business at hand.

"You should have seen the look on her face when she saw those pictures and all those crime reports. She was crying like a little baby when I left."

"That's good, Frank. Now, I want you to go to Dallas in the morning and have a face-to-face meeting with Gerald Parker."

"Sure thing, boss. What do you want me to tell him?"

"Just ask him if he has the money, which we know he doesn't. Then, go back to your hotel and wait. I will let you know what to do next."

"Got it," Jacobson said.

"And Frank."

"Sir?"

"You might not want to take Miss Lacey with you," J. Edward suggested.

"Gotcha!" he said, cocking his thumb and forefinger like a pistol and pointing at him. He walked out of the office, a loaded cannon just waiting for J. Edward to light the fuse.

When he was alone again, J. Edward contemplated how things were starting to come together. He still didn't have a definite date for his shipment from Bolivia, but he was certain things were being worked out. Having sent Jacobson over to see Lisa Dalton should be enough to set Breckenridge up to be taken completely out of the picture. He'd suspected for some time that he was getting entirely too independent and becoming a risk that he didn't need.

Then, there was Gerald Parker, that sniveling worm of a man. J. Edward smiled at the knowledge that he never had the slightest clue that they'd been setting him up all along. He'd even had a hand in seeing that Parker got the prospectus for the floundering gold mining project in

Bolivia, knowing he'd see it as his last shot at pulling himself out of his financial quagmire.

Now, there was only one witness left to the raid on that mining camp — some piss-ant adventurer named Chance. J. Edward still didn't understand why he hadn't been killed. They'd killed everyone else but Parker, and they were supposed to let him live, so he'd come back to the States a broken man. He was certain that it wouldn't be a problem much longer since he'd dispatched some of his henchmen down to Bolivia to take care of that last loose end.

CHAPTER 24

IT was four-thirty in the afternoon and Alan Breckenridge had on the same clothes he was wearing when he left La Paz the day before. His suitcases were still by the front door. He sat on the plush carpeting, leaning back against the sofa. His legs were stretched out under the glass coffee table and there was an empty tequila bottle on the floor next to him. He'd chosen tequila because he figured it would get the job done quicker.

All the documents Lisa had dumped out of the file Frank Jacobson had given her were scattered across the table. It was all there. Everything he'd tried to forget, and everything he'd tried to hide, hoping she'd never find out. There were gruesome black and white crime scene photos, images memorializing every horrid detail of what he'd done. The only thing that could have made it worse was if they'd been in color. Then, there were those booking photos from his arrest. Front pose. Side pose. Standing there with a number held up in front of his chest.

Breckenridge tipped the bottle up on end and tried to coax out one last sip. It was empty, so he licked his tongue around the rim for one final taste. He'd started drinking the moment he walked in and found his deepest, darkest secrets scattered across the table. He'd gone into the bedroom and found Lisa's closet empty. She was gone, just like he knew she'd be if she ever found out the truth about his past.

Breckenridge knew there was only one man heartless enough to have done this — J. Edward Adams III. He made a vow right then and there. "Whatever it takes, he'll pay. He'll pay for what he's done to my life. And by God, he'll pay for what he's done to Lisa!" Even in his drunken stupor his words rang clear — his determination was set in stone.

CHAPTER 25

LEANED back and tried to get some sleep. We were only three hours into an eight-hour bus ride, and I was already getting restless. I stretched my legs out under the seat to try and find some relief. I'd pushed the window down to let in a little breeze, but the road was so dry and dusty that it only made things worse. My backpack was stowed under the seat. I had the Beretta 9mm leathered in the holster under my left arm, concealed beneath my khaki bush jacket.

The winding ribbon of road from La Paz to Guanay wasn't one I particularly enjoyed. It spiraled through the Andes Mountains in short stretches of "Russian Roulette Travel", each blind curve just one more spin of the cylinder against the odds of rolling over and careening two-thousand feet into the valley below.

Camino de la Muerte — The Road of Death. More people died in accidents here than on any other road in the world. I'd made this same trip dozens of times over the last few years. Truthfully, I wasn't afraid of the road — but I didn't like the odds. I figured no matter what you did in life, if you spun the wheel of risk enough times your number would eventually come up. It seemed lately that I'd been spinning the wheel an inordinate number of times.

What had me on edge was the job I was going to do. Don Taylor had finally laid out the plan and provided me with a comprehensive intel dossier. I studied every detail and memorized all the pertinent facts. This assignment was going to be considerably more involved than the one I'd carried out on Ramiro Dueñas.

I rode along in the rattle-trap old bus, feeling the heavy weight of destiny on my shoulders. It was a burden I was learning to live with.

CHAPTER 26

GERALD Parker sat alone in the windowless interview room. Even though he knew he was doing the right thing by being there, he still felt like a criminal. It was one more of life's unnerving experiences he would have rather done without.

He'd explained everything to his wife the night before, telling her all of the excruciating details about how he'd borrowed money to keep the business afloat, and how the economic tides had swamped over the bow faster than he could bail it out. He'd even told her about the call from Frank Jacobson, and the veiled threats he'd made about her. Then, he told her what he believed he needed to do.

"Gerald, it's the right thing to do," she'd said.

He thought about how lucky he was to have a wife like her.

"Mr. Parker," said one of the three FBI agents who'd walked into the room. "We want you to start from the very beginning." They were giving him orders before they even sat down. "Tell us when it was you were first contacted by Frontier Financial Corporation, who contacted you, and every event as it unfolded from there. Do you understand?"

"Yeah, okay," Parker said in a weak voice. He pushed a thick stack of files across the table. It was the record of all his dealings with the company.

"We'll get to that later," one of the agents said, pushing back the files. "For now, just tell us the story."

Two of the agents sat on the opposite side of the table, one of them fiddling with a video camera. Once they started recording, they explained the procedure they would follow during the interview.

Parker nodded his head, but his ears were ringing, and he didn't really hear much of what was being said.

"Mr. Parker!" one of them snapped. "You can't just sit there and nod your head. You have to speak up. Understand?"

"Yeah, I got it."

"Fine, then start from the very beginning."

Parker was told that the third agent in the room had been sent down from Oklahoma City to sit in on the interview because that was where Frontier Financial had their main offices. He remained silent, leaning back in his chair, sipping stale coffee from a Styrofoam cup, taking in every word. He was thinking about the bundles of cash he'd get when he brought this latest tidbit of news back to J. Edward Adams III.

CHAPTER 27

THE bus pulled into Guanay in just under nine hours, still in one piece. The cylinder of odds had spun one more time and the hammer dropped on an empty chamber.

I had my gear piled on the bed and peeled off layers of dusty clothes, getting ready to walk down to the hotel's only shower. It would probably be the last one I'd get until this ordeal was over.

The Hotel Panorama isn't much, but it's relatively clean, and has an oscillating fan in each room. It's a simple courtyard layout, honeycombed with small, no-frills rooms, each with a single bed, a wooden table, and a chair. There's one bathroom and a shower that's used by all of the guests.

Guanay can be unbearably hot, and this was one of those sweltering occasions. To try and make things a little more tolerable, I stood naked on the small concrete pad, straddling the drain and dipping one scoop after the other of rainwater from a blue fifty-five-gallon drum. Locally referred to as a "bucket bath", it isn't much, but it's a hell of a lot better than bathing in a muddy river and having to keep a wary eye out for caimans or anacondas.

After I finished cleaning up, I stretched out on the bed in my room and pulled a long drag off an Astoria cigarette. They're unfiltered, harsh-smelling, and sell for about twenty-cents a pack.

I can't believe Don Taylor got me smoking again, I thought. I suppose it's easier to blame it on him than to chalk it up to the real culprit — an avalanche of stress.

I had a thin towel tied around my waist and my wet hair pulled back into a short ponytail. The fan at the foot of the bed blew cool air and dried the last remnants of my "bucket bath" — Third World air conditioning at its finest.

I rubbed a hand across my face, feeling the rough stubble of four day's growth. Wearing my hair longer and only shaving once a week helped keep me from looking like a DEA agent, or any other kind of government man. Being mistaken for either one could be a death sentence out here on the frontier.

I blew a long stream of smoke toward the ceiling and watched the fan whirl it around the room. No escape. It was a lot like I felt about my own situation.

I'd intentionally left La Paz several days early so I could stop at points along the way, validating my cover by inspecting legitimate dredge-mining prospects. I knew that if I went straight into my target, it might arouse suspicion. The natives who live in these remote regions might not be well educated by the world's standards, but they're masters at survival, and if they suspect you're invading their territory for unacceptable reasons, chances of getting out alive are slim to none. A man can disappear in the jungle in more ways than one.

CHAPTER 28

J. EDWARD was extremely pleased with how things were coming together. He'd sent one of his men to Breckenridge's condo to see what was going on since he'd gotten back from Bolivia and was informed that the results were just as he'd hoped. Breckenridge had returned to find his personal life in shambles, and just as J. Edward expected, he'd crash and burned emotionally. If he was lucky, maybe he'd prove how weak he truly was and take his own life. But what pleased him most was the correspondence he held in his hand.

Security problem solved.

Production back online.

Delivery expected within 15 days

Zorro

Only a few short lines, but they spoke volumes. *Zorro* was the Spanish word for fox, and Ramiro Dueñas had used it as his signature on clandestine correspondence. Apparently, Colonel Zoto had picked up the moniker and was carrying on the tradition.

It was just as well as far as J. Edward was concerned. Dueñas had the connections, passion, and ruthless ambition, but he'd gotten a little too slick for J. Edward's tastes. Plus, he was beginning to show signs that the money was making him soft. Colonel Zoto was cut more from the cloth J. Edward preferred — crude, decisive, and ruthless.

Dueñas had obviously made a grave mistake somewhere along the line and it cost him his life. J. Edward was just glad that it happened in the initial stages of their dealings. However inconvenient this transition might be, it was easier to deal with now than it would have been after their business was in full swing.

CHAPTER 29

DON Taylor was back in his Georgetown apartment. It was just as easy to monitor Chance's movements from there as it would have been if he'd stayed in Bolivia. He maintained open contacts in all the intelligence communities, so he'd know immediately if there were any unusual reports from the area where Chance was operating.

Taylor had lived like a fugitive for too many years — always a passport in his pocket. Sometimes he wondered what it would have been like if he'd gotten married and had a family. Even for an old warhorse like him, it tugged at his heart every now and then. He recalled a line from the movie *Heat*. It was something Robert DeNiro's tough-guy character had said: "Don't let yourself get attached to anything you're not willing to walk out on in thirty seconds flat if you feel the heat around the corner." He thought about how true that had been in his own life — how long he'd lived with the "heat" always lurking just around the corner.

Contrary to what people who knew him believed, Taylor still had some feelings of sentimentality, even if he'd resigned himself a long time ago to the fact that his profession wasn't conducive to any worthwhile, lasting relationship. Certainly, he'd enjoyed the company of good women on occasion, and knew several wonderful candidates who'd done all they could to convince him to try and settle down. He'd led them all to believe that he was a successful private security consultant

who worked for multi-national corporations. That helped explain his
odd hours, travel habits, and his almost obsessive commitment to staying in top physical condition. But at this stage in his life, he was basically
a loner, and generally felt stunted in social situations. He felt incomplete
when he was away from the action.

He situated himself in the chair behind his desk and punched the
power switch on his laptop. While he waited for the computer to boot
up, he perused the stack of mail that had accumulated since he'd been
gone. Mostly junk mail addressed to "Current Occupant", but he still
considered each item carefully.

His apartment was in a small nondescript complex in a decent
middle-class neighborhood, in line with maintaining his low-profile
lifestyle. In his office he had a desk, laptop, printer, scanner, and all the
other standard workaday necessities. On the credenza behind him he
kept a coffeemaker and an mp3 player loaded with his favorite music. At
least that helped break the monotony and silence that came with working long, lonely hours.

On the other side of the room was where he kept his exercise
equipment. There was a compact set-up with various lengths of resis-
tance bands, a sit-up board, a heavy bag mounted from the ceiling, and
a chin-up bar that spanned the width of the doorway. Along with a nice
stretch of residential street for long morning jogs, he had everything a
man needed to stay in top form.

Just as his laptop booted up, the answer struck him like a bolt
of lightning.

"Son-of-a-bitch!" He slammed his palm flat on the desk. It was the
only place it could have come from — the one that rolled over on Chance.

But how? And more importantly, why? Taylor knew the "how"
and the "why" could be solved easily enough. He just hoped Chance
survived that long.

CHAPTER 30

FRANK Jacobson arrived in Dallas around three in the afternoon. He hadn't flown because of the specialized equipment he needed to bring with him. It was only a three-hour drive, but it still bored the hell out of him. Actually, it had taken him over four hours because he'd stopped at a XXX adult store just across the Texas border to pick up some "amorous accessories" for Lacey. Always the gentleman.

Jacobson drove along Northwest Highway, rubbernecking in search of suitable entertainment. He believed Dallas to be the "titty-bar" capital of the world and was searching for a club he'd visited the last time he was in town.

He crawled along at about ten miles per hour, trying to get a better look. So far, he'd ignored the honks of irritated drivers stacking up behind him. He hoped some brave soul might make a fool-hearted attempt and confront him. At least then he'd have the opportunity to blow off a little steam.

"Hot damn, there it is!" He saw the club he'd been looking for and swung over into the left-hand turn lane, waiting for a break in the traffic so he could scoot across into the crowded lot. A blue Ford pickup pulled up behind him. The driver believed that Frank had missed an opportunity to cross and began hammering his fist on the horn. Jacobson glanced up in his rearview mirror and saw the man frantically waving his arms and mouthing what he was sure were not kind words. He tapped the power button and the driver's side window slid down. Sure enough, he could hear ranting and raving that dealt with everything from his sexual preferences to casting aspersions on his mother's moral character. To top it all off, the guy was smirking to a girl seated next to him, like maybe Jacobson wouldn't have the *cajones* to get out and confront him.

His meeting with Gerald Parker wasn't until the next morning, so he decided to have a little fun, and just sat there while several wide spaces opened up in the oncoming traffic where he could have easily pulled across to the other side.

Just as he anticipated, the guy went ballistic, honking, screaming, and flailing his arms again. Then, much to Jacobson's pleasure, he got out of his truck.

One of the perks he'd been given working for Frontier Financial was they provided him with a company car. It was a full-size, four-door Lincoln Continental. Not only did the vehicle enhance his fantasy of being an executive, but it also helped to disguise his massive size.

He waited until the irate driver got even with the trunk of his Lincoln, and then kicked open the door and started unwinding out of the car. His attacker-to-be caught a glimpse of his size as he cleared the roofline and executed a mid-stride pivot that would make an NFL halfback proud, racing back to his truck. He jumped inside the cab and slammed the door, locking it in the same swift motion.

The girl sitting next to him, who had been swooning at his previous bravado, was terrified. "Back it up, back it up, back the damn truck up!" she pleaded, slapping him on the shoulder with each frantic demand.

The driver glanced in the rearview mirror and saw that someone had pulled in behind them. They were trapped.

Jacobson knew when he got up that morning that he didn't have any meetings scheduled, so he'd dressed for comfort. He had on a pair of oversized black gym pants, and a red T-shirt that was stretched across his massive chest. And of course, there were his freakishly muscular arms. His "big guns", as he liked to call them. The enormous gut that pushed out in front of him only added to his fearsome bulk.

Jacobson walked up to the driver's side window and glared in at the panicked occupants. "Got a problem, cowboy?" he asked.

"No sir...I'm sorry sir...I didn't mean to..." The guy was horrified, and his voice was little more than a muffled whimper through the glass.

"Yeah, that's kind of what I thought." Jacobson grinned. "But in case you forget." He hooked his thumbs into the waistband of his gym pants and pulled them down, whipping out the one part of his anatomy that others had always assumed held the bulk of his intelligence. Then, he proceeded to piss all down the side of the man's truck.

The girl slapped her palm across her gaping mouth and elbowed her boyfriend in the ribs. "Are you just going to let him do that?"

"Shut up!" he said. "He can come in here and piss all over you if he wants. I just want to get the hell out of here before he really gets mad."

Jacobson "wiggled his willie", pissing figure eights all down the side of the truck, declaring, "When you gotta' go, you gotta' go." He roared in laughter.

After a minute he loaded himself back into his pants and swaggered over to his car. He slid in and stomped on the accelerator, fishtailing through the oncoming traffic and into the parking lot of the club. This was turning out to be one sweet day.

CHAPTER 31

ALAN Breckenridge was mentally lost. He still had on the same wrinkled clothes he'd left La Paz in a few days before. It didn't matter much in the company he was keeping now. In fact, he looked about as good as everyone else in the joint.

He'd stumbled in around eight o'clock that morning. The Wagon Wheel, or Wagon Rut, or something like that. He didn't remember for sure. It wasn't important. He knew they were serving booze, and that was all that mattered. He remembered seeing the place before when he'd driven through the Stockyards area of Oklahoma City. Back then it disgusted him. He wondered what kind of man would be drinking that early in the morning. But today, his heart skipped a beat of happiness when he saw that string of colorful lights flashing around the front door and knew they were open for business.

He'd staggered in and almost fell off the backless barstool. The place smelled like dirty drains, mold, and depression. It was perfect for the mood he was in.

"Straight up, barkeep," he said.

"Cash up front," the grizzled old man demanded, and Breckenridge slid a crisp hundred-dollar bill across the bar.

Now, there was a row of eight empty shot glasses staring back at him. He still didn't feel any better. His mind was muddled in alcohol, and although he wasn't even sure what day it was, there was one thought that remained crystal clear in his mind. *J Edward is going to pay for what he's done to me. What he's done to Lisa. What he's done to us.*

CHAPTER 32

SPECIAL Agent Donaldson was back in his office. His trip to sit in on Gerald Parker's interview in Dallas had been a real eye opener. Parker had some solid information. A lot of it was circumstantial, but there was enough that he knew they might try and put a case together. He knew Parker's confession could crack the lid on a rancid sewer that would stink up his own backyard, and he couldn't let that happen.

"Do you really think they can make a case out of this?" his partner asked, flipping through the interview transcript. "Most of these accusations are pretty wild, and even if this Jacobson guy is the thug he's trying to make him out to be, it doesn't mean that J. Edward Adams III is involved in what he's doing?"

"I know," Donaldson agreed. "But stranger things have happened." In the back of his mind he was thinking, *If you had any clue as to what was really going on, you'd know that J. Edward is more than just involved — he's calling the shots.*

"Do you have any idea what kind of political clout this Adams guy has? Hell, if we go after him and we're wrong, we'll be spending the rest of our careers in some field office out on the Alaskan tundra, investigating lint balls rolling around behind the filing cabinets."

"Yeah, we'd better wait and see what happens before we start anything too serious," Donaldson said. He turned his attention back to some notes on another case they were working on. What he was really focused on was how J. Edward was going to react when he found out what Gerald Parker was up to.

CHAPTER 33

I **ARRIVED** in Mapiri early afternoon. Just as I had in Guanay, I planned on spending the night before moving closer to the staging area for my assignment. I wanted to be seen by as many people as possible who might remember me from my past work in the area.

It didn't take long to attract a crowd. After sitting in the town plaza for less than an hour, dozens of young men came up to me, two and three at a time. They all had the same agenda. "Do you need workers, *don* Chance? I've got lots of experience and I know a secret place along the river that has never been worked before by anyone except a very close friend of mine, and he found much gold there."

Their stories were all the same and I've heard them a hundred times before. They all professed to have years of mining experience and knew exactly where the mother lode could be found. The truth was, there were very few who really knew where any gold was, and if they did, they would have already worked the area themselves. Bottom line: They were desperate for work and would say anything they thought might help them get a job. I certainly couldn't fault them for that.

As potential workers continued to approach, I feigned interest in their stories, making notes in a small spiral notebook. I asked questions about location, water depth, currents, access, and all the other details I'd need to know if I really were considering a new site. I assured them I'd think about their offers and explained that I was leaving town tomorrow morning to inspect an area I was already interested in. I promised that if things worked out, I'd be back to hire a crew. I knew if anyone came around asking, rumor that I was back in business prospecting for gold would spread like wildfire, and that's just what I wanted.

Too many foreigners had come through this area before, taken what they could from these trusting people, and left town owing salaries and debts for gasoline and other supplies. I'd always made it a point to treat my crew fairly, pay them well, and never leave a debt unsettled. Because of that investment in basic decency before, I was reaping the rewards now. People around here remembered me, and more importantly, they trusted me.

I sat down at a small open-air cafe to have a bite to eat. I waved at the only policeman in town to come over and join me. It never hurt to have a friend with the keys to the jail — and a gun.

CHAPTER 34

J. **EDWARD** wasn't mad, but he was irritated. There was another leak in the damn, and one he'd have to plug pretty quick. Things were moving along too smoothly at this point to have any additional obstacles thrown in the way. He knew the caller was somewhere out in public because he could hear traffic and the general ruckus of crowd noise in the background. He also knew the man would never risk calling from his office.

"Mr. Adams, there is a serious problem brewing with one of your clients — a Gerald Parker."

"And?" He gave the man his undivided attention.

"He's spoken to the FBI in Dallas about what he believes were threats made to him and his family by one of your men."

"Do you know who the complaint was about?"

"It was Frank Jacobson."

"Was he taken seriously?"

"Enough so that a full-blown investigation could very well be started. They're going to need more information and they've already scheduled him for another interview."

"That is unfortunate," J. Edward said. "As usual, I am sure you will find me quite grateful for your efforts."

Agent Donaldson thought about the prospect of more of J. Edward's "generosity". It would certainly help boost his secret retirement fund, but it wasn't doing much for his nerves. He knew he was taking an even greater risk now than he ever had in the past.

The proverbial limb was thin, and the wind was beginning to blow. He knew it was time for one last play. Then, he'd cash in and get the hell out of Dodge.

CHAPTER 35

DON Taylor followed his hunch and it led him to a conclusion he knew was going to leave a bad taste in his mouth. He believed men who abused the trust that comes with wearing a badge were some of the most despicable vermin there were. Men like that were often smart, but usually too smart for their own good. They darted out to nibble away at the very foundation of decency. But this rodent hadn't been smart enough, and he'd left a trial of droppings that were leading Taylor right to him. The trap was being set and Taylor was preparing to slam it shut, right across his scrawny neck.

"That's right. I need phone records, bank statements, credit card charges, listings of assets — the works," Taylor said. Now, he had two suspects, and before long he knew he'd have the guilty one in his crosshairs.

"I can have it all to you in four or five days," the research assistant said.

"That won't cut it. I need it in twenty-four hours," Taylor demanded.

"But that's…"

Taylor killed the connection. He knew the rest of what the man was going to say would include the word "impossible", and that wasn't something he was interested in hearing.

CHAPTER 36

ALAN Breckenridge had spent the night in his car. He forced his eyes open slowly, tumbling hard into a new morning. Even the slightest movement started the pounding in his head.

He reached for the bottle on the passenger side floorboard and tilted it to his lips. Empty. He pitched it out the open window. Glass shattered on the sidewalk.

While struggling to sit up in the driver's seat he got a first glimpse of himself in the rearview mirror. Several days growth of beard shadowed his pale face. Dark circles underscored his eyes, and even though they were only half open, he could still see the red lines running through them, mapping the road of physical destruction that he'd put his body through over the last few days. Breckenridge was a victim to the reverse metamorphosis that alcohol could do to a man — butterfly to cocoon to worm.

As dull as his thoughts were, one spark still flickered bright. He would not let J. Edward get away with what he'd done. The hammer slammed even harder against the anvil, but this time the pain wasn't in his head. It was in his heart.

CHAPTER 37

I GOT up before sunrise and prepped my gear, getting ready for the next leg of the journey. The standard mode of transportation out of Mapiri was standing room only in the back of a small Toyota pickup. There were always too many passengers packed into the bed of the truck, and even thinking about trying to get enough room for yourself to sit down was wasted effort. At 0500 I claimed my square-foot of space and rolled out of town with the rest of the travelers, heading for Yuyo.

After about two hours, we passed through the roadside village of Achiquiri. It was little more than a handful of bamboo huts stretched out along the dirt road. We stopped long enough to wedge in one or two more passengers, and then moved on for the last few hours of the trip. There was a small store at the edge of town, and I gave serious consideration to jumping off and trying to grab a cold drink, but knew if I did, I might not be able to jam myself back into the bed of the truck. I decided it was best to tough it out and ride dry and thirsty.

Along the rest of the route, we stopped at various points to let passengers off. They unloaded sacks of flour, tin cans of cooking oil, and whatever other necessities they couldn't take directly from the land and had to travel into town to buy. Then, they would thread themselves and their cargo along the narrow paths, disappearing into the jungle.

Somewhere hidden beyond that imposing emerald wall was the simple world they called home.

It's easy for people to sit back and sneer down their noses, pointing out all of the things these people don't have. But one thing you do have to admire is their resourcefulness and resilience.

The road finally curved around to the opposite side of the mountain, and far below in the cupped hands of the valley I could see the small village of Yuyo. It was beautiful in its rustic simplicity, and I felt a chill of happiness like one gets coming home.

Cristina and I lived in Yuyo for several wonderful months. We had a bamboo hut high on the side of the hill, giving us a panoramic view of the main camp down below. For all that time my crew and I mined for gold in the river that ran alongside the village. Many of those same workers that shared their lives with us here, followed us back to Chulumani and were killed in the raid on our camp. Consequently, that pleasant feeling of homecoming was mingled with the bitter taste of sadness.

The Toyota stopped at the edge of the river. I slung my pack over one shoulder, and then picked up the 12-gauge and hopped down. I was the only one staying in Yuyo. The rest of the passengers would go across the river via balsa raft, load into the back of another pickup waiting on the other side and travel the rest of the way to Apolo.

A spot some distance beyond Apolo was my planned destination, but I'd take a much different route getting there. It would be dangerous and physically demanding, but more secure in the long run considering my agenda.

I walked over to a dilapidated thatch-roofed hut that leaned hard to one side. There was a rusty, red and blue tin sign advertising Paceña beer nailed to the front door. I laid down my pack, took a seat on a stump in a small patch of shade, and cradled the shotgun in my lap. I noticed a mangy old mutt with one mangled ear and a nasty-looking raw spot the size of a fist chewed into the back of his neck. I guess he lost the fight. He looked up, decided it wasn't worth the effort to amble over and beg for food, and laid his head back down to go to sleep. A rail-thin native, wearing tattered green soccer shorts and a faded blue Lynyrd Skynyrd T-shirt, ambled barefooted out of the hut.

"*Una cerveza, por favor,*" I said.

He looked about as interested as the old mutt but went back inside to get me a warm bottle of beer. Life can be good in the bush.

CHAPTER 38

F RANK Jacobson got the call from J. Edward the night before. He'd told him that Gerald Parker's account was out of hand and needed to be cancelled. He understood exactly what he was being told to do, and he was thrilled.

He was parked about half a block from Parker's home. Even at this distance he knew he was taking a big risk, but it was one he was willing to accept. Any farther away and he wouldn't have a clear line of sight. Being able to see first-hand the results of his handiwork in action was one of the great pleasures he got from his work. Besides, he wanted to be certain that he got the job done right, because J. Edward had promised him a bonus when it was completed. He didn't have a clue what that surprise might be, but if the big man himself was going to choose it, he knew it would be something special.

Earlier that morning, in the cover of predawn darkness, Jacobson delivered a special surprise of his own to the Parker home. He'd skulked up to the side of the house and let himself into the garage through an unlocked side door and installed it under the chassis of the dark blue Mercedes he knew Parker drove to his office every morning.

The package was small, but deadly. He'd set the detonator with a seven-second delay. Once Parker started the engine, the timer would begin, allowing him plenty of time to back out of the garage and down the driveway. The delay would also ensure that he would be completely sealed inside the car with the door shut. He'd seen a similar job done where the detonator was wired directly to the ignition. The man got in and started the car before he closed the door. He was blown twenty feet out of his vehicle but survived. He couldn't risk making a mistake like that. He had to be certain that Parker was sealed tight inside and all the way down the driveway when the explosion occurred.

• • •

Gerald Parker had gotten up an hour earlier than usual. He'd even punched the button on the alarm clock before it went off. He was nervous, but in an excited and positive kind of way. Today would be difficult, but it was one more step toward validating his courage in doing the right thing. He had an appointment scheduled with Frank Jacobson at eleven o'clock — the same man who'd called his home and threatened him and his family.

"Well, big man, now let's see who's calling the shots," he said to the bathroom mirror, exaggerating his best tough-guy voice. He was beginning to feel his old bravado coming back.

Parker's wife, Janet, slipped up and looped her arms around him from behind. He stood there with a towel wrapped around his waist and his face half-covered with shaving cream. She began nibbling at his ear and twirling her fingers in the hair on his chest.

"Baby, as much as I would *love* to finish what you're starting, I really do need to get ready. You know I've got an early meeting with the FBI, and then I'm meeting with Frank Jacobson after that."

Ever since he'd confided in her about all that had been going on, their relationship changed dramatically. She acted like she was proud of him again, and things were almost like they were when they were first married. He finally felt like he was being the man she deserved. But

Parker hadn't told her about his having hidden in the jungle while innocent people were slaughtered because of his cowardice. He'd decided it might be best to leave that part out.

"Alright," Janet conceded. "But you don't know what you're missing."

"Oh, I *absolutely* know what I'm missing," he said. "And I intend on taking every advantage of it as soon as I get home."

Parker's oldest daughter walked into the bedroom and flopped down on their bed, still wearing her pink Hello Kitty pajamas.

"Grrrr...who's your tiger, baby!" Parker growled, spinning Janet around and wrapping her up in a playful hug. He hadn't noticed his daughter in the bedroom behind them.

"You two!" the little girl squealed. "That's gross!" They all laughed.

Janet walked out of the bathroom and lay on the bed next to their daughter, just as their youngest skipped into the room and jumped up next to her mother and sister.

"Honey, didn't you say something about having some work you needed to finish at the office today?" Janet asked.

"Yeah, but I'll swing by after my meetings and pick up the files and bring them home."

"Oh, no you don't," she objected. "I know how you are. You go by the office and we won't see you until late tonight."

"No, I promise. It won't take more than five minutes. I've got everything boxed up on the desk and ready to go," he said.

"I tell you what," Janet said. "You finish getting ready and have breakfast with the girls, and I'll run down to the office and pick everything up. How does that sound?"

"See girls. What have I always told you? Your mother is an angel."

"Oh, daddy!" they giggled

Parker walked over to the three loves of his life. He reached down and dabbed a dollop of shaving cream onto each of their noses, and then leaned over and kissed his wife on the lips, making an exaggerated smacking sound. The two little girls giggled even harder.

CHAPTER 39

COLONEL Juan Zoto stepped fully into the position left by Ramiro Dueñas and was playing both roles — feared military commander and rising star in the world of *los narcos*. He wasn't sure which gave him the most satisfaction. However, he was sure which one was going to make him the most money.

His military position gave him the means to control many of the circumstances that directly affected his newest endeavor. He was able to influence the UMOPAR patrols that scoured the jungles in search of cocaine production facilities and could easily direct them to areas that wouldn't interfere with his own operations. In fact, he could see to it that they pursued his competitors. But this new role in the hierarchy of *los narcos* intrigued him immensely. He was being invited into social circles he could have only dreamed of before. The "beautiful people", he liked to call them. Plus, he had access to piles of money like he'd never imagined possible since inheriting the multi-million-dollar deposit J. Edward had given to Dueñas, and that was only the tip of the iceberg to come.

Today, Zoto traveled across the border into Peru to make certain everything was in order at the production facility. The first loads of paste had been delivered from the processing operation he and Dueñas had been inspecting when he'd gotten his head blown off.

The men working in camp were noticeably tense. They knew Colonel Zoto's reputation for brutality was much more than just ugly rumors.

"Everything is as you ordered, *mi colonel*," said Enrique, the camp manager. He'd transformed ass-kissing into an art form.

"It appears so," Zoto said. "But we have to be absolutely certain. How many drums of acetone do we have in storage?"

"One hundred, sir, just as you ordered."

After soaking coca leaves in vats of acetone, the runoff liquid, known as *aqua rica*, would be processed into the thick white paste used to make the deadly powder that would fuel his burgeoning empire. Since acetone was tightly controlled in Bolivia to combat illegal drug production, the plan Dueñas had devised was to store the chemicals at the site in Peru, and then after the boats came down river with the paste, they could return to Bolivia carrying loads of the necessary liquid. That way, they wouldn't have to purchase the acetone in Bolivia, and thus give government officials any reason to suspect what they might be up to.

"That should be more than enough," Zoto said. He swaggered around camp, slapping a leather riding crop against his thigh. He idolized the old German SS officers, many of whom had fled to Bolivia after the war. He'd seen the Nazi icons carrying the leather crops in old photos and movies and believed having one bolstered his hardline image.

At the far edge of camp, he spotted something that most certainly wasn't in accordance with his orders for how security was to be handled. One of the sentries was leaned up against the side of a plywood storage shack with his weapon slung casually over his shoulder. He was holding a cigarette with one hand and using the other to punctuate a lively conversation he was having with one of the young girls who worked in the kitchen.

Colonel Zoto marched toward them in long, determined strides. Enrique shuffled along behind him, knowing something unpleasant was about to take place.

"Enjoying yourself, soldier?" Zoto snapped.

The young man turned, and when he saw who it was, the color quickly drained from his face. He flicked the burning cigarette into the bush.

"No sir...yes sir...I mean, I'm sorry, sir." He felt an intense wave of nausea wash through him.

"This is a sentry post, not a social club," Zoto scolded. "How do you expect to guard your area of responsibility if your attention is focused on whether or not this young girl will be in your bunk tonight?" He motioned to the girl with his riding crop.

"Sir, I promise, it will never happen again." He felt the value of his life drop to the price of a pinch of salt.

"You are right, soldier, it will *not* happen again!" Colonel Zoto drew his pistol.

The sentry squeezed his eyes shut and began mouthing a Hail Mary, crossing himself and preparing to die. Every muscle in his body tensed, waiting for the bullet to end it all. But the shot didn't come, and after a moment, he carefully opened his eyes, wondering what was happening.

Colonel Zoto was holding the pistol in his hand, offering it to the young man.

"Sir?" He was confused.

"Soldier, are you committed to our cause and to protecting your post with your life?"

"Sir, yes sir!"

"Then take this weapon and kill the girl who has taken you from your duty," he ordered.

Zoto reached out and grabbed a handful of the girl's long hair to keep her from escaping. She struggled, trying to pull away, but to no avail.

"But sir, I can't..."

Zoto jammed the barrel of the pistol into the man's chest.

"It is her life or yours. Now, make your choice!" he demanded.

The young man took the gun in his shaking hand and aimed it at her head.

The girl dropped to her knees and began sobbing. "Please, don't kill me!" she begged, looking up at the man who only moments before had been an adoring suitor.

"Not there!" Colonel Zoto slapped the sentry's hand, so the barrel of the pistol dropped down and pointed at her stomach. "This way her death will come slowly and be extremely painful. We must make a point so others will not make the same mistake. Now, shoot her!"

The soldier squeezed his eyes shut, forcing out a stream of tears.

The shot rang throughout the camp.

The girl looked up in disbelief and horror, clutching her hands to her stomach, dark blood oozing between her fingers.

Colonel Zoto spun around and faced Enrique. "Tie her to a tree in the middle of camp and let her bleed out. I want everyone to see her die."

"*Si, mi colonel!*" Enrique said, clicking his heels together to accentuate his commitment.

Zoto turned back and took the pistol from the sentry's hand, still dazed and staring down at the girl, agonizing over what he'd just done. "Good work, soldier. Now, return to your duties," he said, holstering the pistol.

The young man said nothing. He slung his rifle from his shoulder and held it at port arms. Then, he turned his back on the girl, dying slowly on the ground.

CHAPTER 40

FRANK Jacobson was getting restless. It was just shy of eight o'clock in the morning and he'd been sitting in his car for almost four hours. He'd arrived long before sunrise to get everything ready. There was no way in hell that he was going to miss the big show, and all this waiting around was getting to be too much.

"Come on already, let's go!" he yelled inside his car.

Now, he was really uncomfortable, realizing he never should have drunk that Big Gulp. He rattled the last of the ice around in the plastic cup, squirming from one position to the other, trying to relieve the pressure on his bladder. He couldn't stand the bitter taste of coffee and thought the huge soda might give him the sugar boost he needed to stay awake. In hindsight, he could see now that it probably wasn't such a good idea after all.

Finally, the garage door started coming up and he could see the red glow of taillights flashing like someone was riding the brake. He adjusted his binoculars to be sure he had the best view.

"I can't wait to see the look on your face, you little wimp," he chortled.

The car backed down the driveway.

"What the hell?" He adjusted the focus on his binoculars to be certain of what he was seeing.

Janet waved back to the house. Gerald Parker was holding their youngest daughter in his arms and they were waving through the front bay window. Their oldest daughter was upstairs in her bedroom, holding back her pink Hello Kitty curtains with one hand, and waving goodbye to her mother with the other.

Then, it happened. The ground rumbled and the Mercedes launched straight up into the air, crashing back to the street with the sickening sound of torn and twisting metal. A ball of flames engulfed the car. Fire shot out from underneath the chassis and scorched the yard. The blast blew leaves off the trees and birds scattered in flight. The deafening explosion shattered windows in houses all up and down the block.

Gerald Parker instinctively threw a forearm across his face and spun away from the window to protect his daughter from the shattering glass, but it didn't shield him from seeing the horror that consumed his wife. He stood there in shock, his mouth stretched wide open to scream, but not a sound came out. His daughter clung to his neck and buried her face in his shoulder.

"Shit, shit, shit!" Jacobson grumbled, slamming his fist against the top of the steering wheel. Then, he carefully pulled away from the curb, driving slowly past the mangled remains of the car, and what had been Parker's wife.

Neighbors who hadn't already left for work began coming out of their houses, horrified at what they saw. Sirens wailed in the distance.

The Parker's oldest daughter stood by her upstairs window. Broken glass was scattered across the floor. Pinpricks of blood dotted her face. Her pink curtains laid torn and tangled at her feet. The morning breeze tousled her blonde hair as she stared at the burning car and the horrific scene of devastation down below.

CHAPTER 41

I SPENT the night in Yuyo, reminiscing with old friends. The village hadn't changed much since the last time I was here, and it probably wouldn't for the next hundred years. The people are poor, but content. They've got a roof over their heads and manage to hunt and gather enough to keep themselves fed. As far as they're concerned, they don't really need much else.

After spending the night camped at the edge of the river, I got up before sunrise and had coffee with a few of the villagers. Then, I hoisted my pack on my shoulder, took my shotgun in hand, and headed down the narrow trail that led into the bush. As I walked away, I raised the 12-gauge over my head in a farewell gesture. Without even turning around, I knew they were waving back, wishing me luck.

• • •

I'd been walking for almost seven hours. The river was low and even though the shoreline was covered with small rocks and boulders, it was still easier going than it would have been having to slash my way through the endless tangle of thick jungle higher up on the bank.

I was making good time, so I stopped at a flat stretch of beach to have a bite to eat. It wasn't much, only a tin of sardines and a canteen of water, but it would be enough.

After lunch, and just like I used to do with my crew every morning in camp, I packed my cheek with a thick wad of coca. The potent little leaves would boost my energy levels enough that I could walk for hours on end, staving off hunger and fatigue. The natural stimulant would be like a hot shot of espresso spread out over a long, grueling day.

A soft breeze blew down through the valley and along the river. It would be nice to be able to take off my sweat-soaked shirt and enjoy the cool air, but then I'd have to contend with thick clouds of yellow, "no-see-um" gnats that would swarm my body, attracted to the salty sweat. I hoisted myself up from the comfortable spot on the beach, shouldered my pack, and picked up my weapon. I spat a long stream of dark green juice from the bitter chaw of coca leaves and resumed my journey.

CHAPTER 42

FRANK Jacobson went straight back to his motel after the disaster at the Parker home. He still hadn't decided how he was going to explain the fiasco to Mr. Adams, but he knew he was going to have to think of something, and quick. Blowing up a suburban housewife in front of her family wouldn't remain a secret for very long. He knew it was probably already a top video on YouTube, Facebook, and all over the local news. *All those sirens…all those neighbors with their damn cell phone cameras. Shit, shit, shit!* He didn't dare turn on the radio for fear of what he'd hear.

Jacobson pulled around to the back of the motel and parked directly in front of his room. He got out and fumbled around in his pocket for the key. When he touched the door, it eased open, already unlocked. He stood up straight and pushed it with the toe of his boot. He squinted, peeking inside the dark room and freezing in place when he saw who was sitting on the edge of his bed.

"What the hell are you doing in my room," he barked in his best tough-guy voice. He wasn't the least bit afraid of who he saw, or disappointed. He just thought the best move was to sound irritated and threatening.

"I'm your bonus, Frank. You know, just like Mr. Adams promised."

"Holy shit!" he said. "Mr. Adams sent you — for me?" His tough guy persona suddenly disappeared.

"Well, are you coming in, or not?" she asked.

"Oh, yeah. Oh, hell yeah!" he said. Without a doubt, this was one of the most beautiful women he'd ever seen. *This ain't no regular rent-a-date,* he thought. *She's long and creamy. Curves in all the right places, and smooth and hard everywhere else. And she's sitting on the edge of my bed, hair wet from a shower. And damn, she's wearing one of my shirts with the buttons undone, waiting for me. Thank you, Mr. Adams — thank you!* His mind turned to erotic mush.

"Well, what do you think, Frank?" she asked seductively.

"Oh, yeah — hell yeah!" he said again.

"How did the job go?"

"What? Oh, yeah, the job." Jacobson tumbled back from his carnal daydream. "Well, there was a little problem," he mumbled.

"Problem?" she asked, digging for details.

"I accidentally blew up his wife."

"What?" That certainly wasn't what she'd expected to hear.

"Yep, blew her up." There, he'd said it.

"And Gerald Parker?"

"Nope, he's still alive. Him and those two kiddos watched the whole thing."

She couldn't believe what she was hearing and knew that J. Edward would be livid. "It's alright, Frank. Sometimes things happen," she said calmly. "Why don't you go take a shower, and I'll be right here waiting for you when you're done."

"You mean…you mean I still get you…get my bonus?" He couldn't believe his luck.

The woman stood up slowly from the bed. Her shirt swung open and exposed her breasts. She stretched up on her tiptoes and kissed him on the tip of his chin, her nipples brushing across his chest. "It'll be okay, Frank. Mistakes happen. I'll explain things to Mr. Adams. Now, go get cleaned up." She brushed the back of her hand across the swelling front of his slacks.

"You got it, doll! I'll be right back!" Jacobson beamed, heading to the bathroom, whistling a happy tune.

Once the woman heard the water running in the shower, she made the call.

"Yes," he answered.

"There's a problem."

"I know. It's all over the news."

"Any changes?"

"No. Just get it done and get back here as soon as possible."

The line went dead.

J. Edward's plans for Frank Jacobson would go forward as planned. This latest incident only confirmed their necessity.

Jacobson came out of the bathroom, still whistling. The arrival of his bonus had taken his mind off what had happened at the Parker home. He puffed out his chest and dropped the towel to the floor, believing he would impress his visitor.

There she stood. His beautiful surprise. Only now, she was fully dressed, standing with her shoulders squared, her knees slightly bent, holding a stainless-steel Walther PPK .380 pistol aimed straight at him. There was a long silencer screwed onto the front of the weapon.

"What the..." Those were the last words he would ever utter.

Two quick rounds spat out, finding their mark in Jacobson's chest, less than a sixteenth of an inch apart. That stopped his massive body cold. His chin dropped and he coughed twice. She tapped the third round just above the bridge of his nose, blowing out the back of his head, splattering a grotesque piece of bloody artwork all over the bathroom mirror behind him.

Jacobson fell into a naked heap on the tile floor.

She knew the first two rounds had done the job — they were dead center chest shots and his heart had stopped before his mouth dropped open. The third round was just for good measure. She glanced in the bathroom mirror, craning her head to the left so she could get a better look at herself between the blobs of blood and brain matter. She brushed her fingers through her hair, and then dropped the pistol into her purse. She was done. So was Frank Jacobson.

CHAPTER 43

J. **EDWARD** sat on the couch in his office, contemplating the events of the last few days, as well as those things that still needed to happen for his plans to succeed. All indications were that his first shipment from Bolivia would be arriving soon. Alan Breckenridge appeared to be completely out of the picture. He hadn't even had the balls to call the office since his return. And finally, that moron Frank Jacobson was out of his hair for good. Even though he'd always done as he was told, he was getting way too sloppy, and that incident at the Parker home had been the final straw.

J. Edward was most pleased with his newest associate. She was educated, cultured, beautiful, and took to her work with absolutely no emotion. He had often thought it was time to get away from bent-nose muscle like Jacobson. That was the kind of man his father and his cronies had used in the old days. But times had changed. Today's marketplace responded much better to intelligence and style, along with deadly force. He was preparing his organization accordingly.

J. Edward picked up the phone and called the man who'd first alerted him to the problem brewing with Gerald Parker.

"What kind of damage has been caused by the incident that took place in Dallas?" he asked as soon as the call connected.

"Are you out of your mind calling me here?" Agent Donaldson whispered anxiously into the phone. His eyes darted around his office, looking for whoever might be within earshot of their conversation.

"Remember who you are talking to, my friend," J. Edward warned.

"Okay, I'm sorry, but this isn't a good idea."

"Then I will be brief," J. Edward said. "Has our problem escalated?"

"Hell, yes it's escalated," Donaldson heavy-whispered, still looking around to make sure he wasn't being overheard. "They blew up his wife, for God's sake."

"Then contact me as soon as you have any updates. That is, unless you would rather that I call you." He knew the slight threat would be understood.

"Give me until tomorrow. I should know what's going on by then," Donaldson said, hanging up the phone and nervously chewing on his thumbnail.

"Hey, what's the deal with all the whispering?" his partner asked, walking around the corner of his cubicle and surprising him. "Got some new little sweetie you haven't told me about?"

Agent Donaldson startled, biting close at his nail and tearing into the quick. "No, nothing like that," he stammered, nervously. He sucked at the blood on his thumb, trying to decide what to do next.

CHAPTER 44

DON Taylor sat at the desk in his Georgetown apartment, perusing through the mass of information he'd requested. It had all come to him in less than twenty-four hours. He scrutinized every detail — every phone call, bank deposit, and credit card charge. Finally, he tapped his finger on the screen at one of the entries. He'd seen the same pattern three times so far. All three calls made to the same number, and all three times a corresponding deposit made into a bank account in Belize.

"I've got you now, you son-of-a-bitch!" he said. "Let's see if you can explain this, but not over the phone — in person!"

Unless the FBI had started handing out twenty-thousand-dollar performance bonuses, Taylor was certain he'd found the rat.

That was the good news, but he was still worried about Chance. He hadn't heard a single word from him or any of his intel sources in Bolivia about his movements. That could mean he still hadn't made contact with his target, or that something bad had happened and he never would.

CHAPTER 45

I COULD feel myself getting back into the rhythm of operating in the jungle. I'd had a few days of sore muscles and stiff joints from pushing myself at an exhausting pace, but my body was starting to flow with the work. One of the most difficult things I had to adjust to was the constant change in terrain. One minute, I might be scrambling over smooth, river-worn boulders. Then, I could be trudging through soft sand, or wading waist-deep against a stiff current in the river. Shortly after that, I might have to slash through jungle so thick I could hardly breathe, and just as I broke through the brush there might be a slope so steep that I'd have to pull myself up by grabbing at sharp rock outcroppings or tangled vines. It was a hellish task, and one that took its toll on the toughest of men. But I'd been here before and knew what it took to survive — strength of mind and a determined heart. The truth was, I felt good here, like it was where I belonged.

I was two days out of Yuyo, skirting around the edges of Apolo and moving up into a small range of dry hills that bordered the military base where the Murillo Battalion was stationed. I could see the airstrip where the dark green Hercules C-130 was spinning up its propellers, preparing for takeoff. The dirt strip wasn't much, but unless there's a heavy rain, it's enough to handle the flight that comes in from La Paz every Friday morning carrying troops, civilian passengers, and supplies.

Since Apolo is the major supply depo for the region, I decided it would be safer to work my way around the town and not be seen. If I was seen here, I'd be remembered. From here on out, being remembered this close to my target wasn't something in my best interest, and certainly wouldn't do anything to help keep me alive.

CHAPTER 46

"I F I ate that crap my stomach would be on fire for a week," Agent Donaldson said. He was amazed at the enormous pile of onions and the amount of hot sauce his partner slathered onto his taco. He would love to enjoy his the same way, but knew his ulcer would revolt if he even took a whiff of such a spicy concoction.

"If you didn't worry about stuff so damn much you wouldn't have a stomach that looked like Swiss cheese," his partner said. He dabbed a small glob of chili from the corner of his mouth with the knuckle of his thumb and deftly licked it off. "Learn to relax a little," he offered.

Donaldson sucked at his milkshake. There was a chunk of strawberry stuck in the bottom of the straw. "Give me a break!" he grumbled, yanking the straw out of the cup and throwing it out the window.

His partner laughed and scarfed down another spicy bite. He knew his observations about Donaldson were right. He did worry too much. He just didn't have a clue about how much there was for him to worry about.

CHAPTER 47

HOMICIDE Detective Lincoln Mayberry was assigned to investigate the murder of Frank Jacobson. He'd also caught the call on the bombing at the Parker house, but as soon as he'd gotten to the scene, the FBI and ATF swooped in and began arguing about jurisdiction and who would be the lead agency. Detective Mayberry knew it would be a lost cause to get into the middle of that pissing contest, so he left a young investigator on scene and told him to let him know when the "alphabet soup gang" decided who'd be calling the shots.

Nobody knew that before Lincoln Mayberry became a detective, and before Gerald Parker's life spiraled into the quagmire that it had become, the two men had been high school buddies. They'd lost touch over the years, but the bonds of friendship built in high school have an unusual way of lasting a lifetime. When Parker called and told him about Frank Jacobson's threats against him and his family, it was the first time they'd spoken in years.

"Listen, Gerald, I really am sorry about what happened," Mayberry said. "I never got the chance to meet Janet, but I'm sure she was a very special lady."

Parker looked at his old friend. They were sitting in a booth at the back of a Denny's restaurant. Mayberry told him when he called that he really shouldn't be talking about the case, but what the hell, they were friends.

"They don't even know if they're going to be able to..." Parker's voice began breaking up. "They couldn't even find all of her body," he said.

"I know, Gerald. It's a helluva' bad deal. I wish there was something I could do to help you get through this."

"Damnit, Lincoln! I know who did it. It was that man I told you about — Frank Jacobson. I should have handled it myself instead of going to the FBI like you told me to do." Parker was lashing out at his old friend.

"I guess you haven't heard," Mayberry said.

Parker's face softened. "Heard what?"

"Frank Jacobson is dead. Someone capped his sorry ass in a motel over on Harry Hines Boulevard."

Parker didn't say a word. He just nodded his head, taking in the news.

"When I know more, you'll know more. Okay?"

"Thanks, Lincoln. You're a good friend," Parker said. "I know you're sticking your neck out talking to me about this, and I really do appreciate it." He grabbed a handful of napkins and wiped them across his face. His eyes were red and swollen and the course paper didn't help. "And I'm sorry that I snapped at you like that. I'm just..."

"Don't worry about it," Mayberry said, taking a handkerchief out of his pocket and handing it to his friend. "The feds don't like us local-yokels crashing their party, but they don't sign my paycheck, so screw 'em. I'll keep poking around and see what I can find out. But for now, let's just keep this where it is — between old friends."

"You know, the girls are still over at my folks' place. They haven't said a word since it happened, and my little one still hasn't stopped crying. I need to get back to them." His voice started breaking up as he slid out of the booth.

Mayberry stayed seated, letting him walk off with a little dignity. "Call me if you need me," he said.

Parker nodded his head. Sobs razored through his heart.

Mayberry could see his old friend's shoulders shaking from behind, knowing he was about to let loose with another torrent of tears.

CHAPTER 48

J. **EDWARD** had his cup full — full of his own self-importance, threatening to spill over the rim. He was entertaining a special guest in his home this evening, and one he very much wanted to impress.

Dominique LeDeaux was a woman who greatly interested him. He just couldn't decide which of her intoxicating qualities appealed to him the most. She was beautiful, intelligent, classically educated, and deadly. He'd never met a woman like her, and she was his newest employee. At least that's how he viewed their relationship. She'd told him she was an independent contractor and worked for no one exclusively, but he was certain he could persuade her otherwise.

"Dominique, are you absolutely certain that I couldn't interest you in a drink? I have an excellent wine cellar, and I'm sure we could find something to your liking."

She let out a slow breath of exasperation, trying to control herself, but her frustration was evident. "Mr. Adams…"

"Please, call me Edward," he interrupted. "There is no need to be so formal."

"Mr. Adams," she said coldly. "First of all, as I have told you, I would prefer that you address me as Ms. LeDeaux. And as I have also told you, I do not drink."

J. Edward passed a snifter of brandy under his nose, saying nothing in response to her comments. She was brash, almost to the point of being insolent, and it intrigued him immensely. "I don't normally socialize with my clients," she said. "The only reason I agreed to this meeting is because of the matter of my payment, and you insisted that it be handled here in person, at your home. Now, might we please settle our business?"

"Ms. LeDeaux," he nodded, hoping she would recognize his respect to address her more formally. "Surely there must be some way I could convince you to work for me on a full-time basis. I assure you, it would be a most rewarding arrangement."

Dominique LeDeaux rose gracefully from the sofa. Her black silk skirt fell down the length of her legs, shaping itself to her impressive form. She was danger personified — a glamorous temptress whose beauty was something you would expect to see in the pages of fashion magazines. But there was nothing glamorous in her tone of voice.

"Mr. Adams, my money, and nothing else," she demanded.

"But surely…" It was a sentence he immediately realized he never should have begun.

In one quick, fluid motion, Dominique LeDeaux swept a dainty pistol from her sequined handbag, pressing it to his forehead. There was nothing dainty about her intentions. "The run-around is over. I expect my payment right this minute, or I will complete my next assignment for absolutely nothing. I will do it right here, and right now, and purely for my own personal satisfaction. Do you understand?"

J. Edward was more impressed with her than ever, but he was not amused at the situation. "Certainly," he agreed. He stepped back from the touch of cold steel, walking down the hallway to his private office. She followed closely behind, the small pistol held at her side, brushing against her silk skirt.

J. Edward leaned over a computer and tapped the keys, printing off a receipt for the international wire transfer. Then, he picked up the document and handed it to her. He held on for a second longer than necessary, causing her to have to tug it from his fingertips. "You can't fault a man for only wanting the best," he said.

"Should you need my services again, you know how to reach me," she said, dropping the receipt into her handbag, along with the pistol. "But next time, it will be payment up front, and no face-to-face contact."

Oh, my God, she is incredible, J. Edward thought. Never in his life had he met a woman who would stand up to him like that.

"Good evening, Mr. Adams," she said, turning on her heel and flowing out of the room.

Dominique LeDeaux had been referred to J. Edward by one of his father's old associates. "She's the best I've ever seen," he'd said. J. Edward had to agree with his assessment. The man who'd recommended her was one of the few from the family business who would still speak to him. The others had written him off a long time ago.

J. Edward thought about how everything would have to work out now. He'd burned too many bridges to ever go back.

CHAPTER 49

D ON Taylor sat in the front seat of his rented Ford Taurus in the parking lot of the Stone Horse Club. He cranked the window down about three inches and reached over to drop open the ash tray. He immediately noticed the bright red plastic plug where the cigarette lighter should have been. "Damn political correctness," he mumbled.

He studied the patrons going inside. By the cars they drove, the clothes they wore, and the way they carried themselves, he got the impression they were hard-working, blue-collar men and women. They looked to be proud, decent people, but had that beat-down look that comes from working too many hours and getting paid far too little for far too long.

He watched the man he'd come to see go in the front door about an hour ago, dressed to the nines. But he still looked like a Fed. That was hard to hide.

Must teach a class at Quantico — Shithead 101, he thought.

It was time. He slid out of the car, slamming the door closed behind him.

• • •

"Come on, sweet thing, let's get out of here and have us a little party of our own," Agent Donaldson slurred.

"Fuck off, grandpa!" the girl said. She flicked cigarette ashes in his lap and exaggerated rolling her eyes as she walked away. She was the fifth girl who'd shot him down so far, but he believed in the power of persistence. Besides, he had a pocket full of cash he couldn't tell anyone about, so he might as well and try and have a little fun. And tonight, he wasn't Special Agent Donaldson with the FBI. He was just plain old "Donny".

"Grandpa? Hell, I'm not that old!" he said. The more he thought about it, the more irritated he got. "Bitch!" he hollered, but the girl was already long gone.

"Hit me again, he said to the bartender. He rattled the ice in his plastic cup, wanting to be sure he had the man's attention. He looked around the club and noticed that he was the only one drinking liquor. Everyone else seemed satisfied with beer.

"How's the action, slick?" the man behind him asked.

"Can't keep their hands off of me," he lied. "They think I'm…" His mouth slammed shut in mid-sentence when he turned around and saw who it was.

"What's the matter? Forget your line?" Taylor asked.

What do you…why are you…?"

Taylor stepped forward and clamped down on Donaldson's crotch with a vice-like grip. He grimaced and dropped his drink. Ice and bourbon spilled across the top of the bar.

"You've got two choices. Get up and follow me out of here so we can talk or die where you sit." He clamped down even harder.

"Okay, okay, you psycho! Let go of me!"

"At least you've got the right idea about who you're dealing with," Taylor said. He eased his grip on the man's nuts. "Now, let's go," he ordered.

The two men walked out the front door. Donaldson limped. Taylor was right behind him.

"Around back," Taylor ordered.

Donaldson turned and looked over his shoulder. The crotch grip had sobered him up a bit and he was beginning to get his confidence back. The blue neon sign hanging over the club entrance cast an eerie glow on both men's faces.

"Before you even think about going for that piece you've got holstered under your jacket, think again," Taylor said. "You'll be dead before you hit the pavement."

Donaldson considered the threat. He didn't know if Taylor had a gun or not but got the distinct impression he might not need one to make good on his threat. "What are we doing back here?" he asked, as they cornered the back of the building.

Taylor swept in and scooped the .38 revolver out of Donaldson's holster. Then, he slammed him face-first against the side of a steel dumpster, hitting it with enough force to slide it back several inches on its iron wheels. He flicked open the pistol and dumped the shells out on the ground and pitched the gun up on the roof of the building. "Now, we're both unarmed," he said. "Want to make a move, or start telling me your story?"

"I don't know what the hell you think you're after, but…"

Taylor used the bottom of his fist like a hammer and smashed Donaldson's nose in a lightning-quick strike. The sounds of crushing bone and cartilage filled his head and bursts of bright light flashed behind his eyes. He stumbled back a couple of steps and dropped to his knees.

"Strike one!" Taylor said. "Cut the bullshit and start telling me who you're involved with, or I promise, strikes two and three will be a lot worse.

Donaldson rocked back off his knees and sat in a puddle of something he could only hope was water but stunk to the high heavens. He leaned against the side of the dumpster, cupping his face in his hands. Blood bubbled out of his busted nose. He was completely sober now. Intense pain has a strange way of doing that to a man. He was certain he didn't want Taylor to "strike him out". He also didn't want to think about the consequences of telling him the truth. He was definitely in a no-win situation. "Look, he said, in a nasal voice. "I don't…"

Another sentence cut short. Taylor snapped a blinding fast kick that grazed the side of his head and tore the bottom of his right earlobe loose. Donaldson grunted a muffled squeal.

"I don't want to hear anything out of your mouth that starts with the words I don't, or I can't, or anything else that makes me think you're holding back on me.

Donaldson held one hand to his smashed nose and the other to the side of his head. "Shit! Yeah, okay!" He was certain now that Taylor would kill him if he didn't tell him what he wanted to know. Better to live now and deal with the rest of it later, he reasoned.

"I'm waiting," Taylor said.

"Adams. J. Edward Adams III. That's the man you want."

"Now, we're on the right track. Enlighten me further. Who is this Adams guy and what's he got to do with Chance?" Taylor struck out with another sharp kick, burying his foot deep into the man's gut.

"What in the hell was that for?" Donaldson sputtered. I'm telling you what you want to know." He laid curled up on his side in the stinking alley.

"Foul ball. Keep talking," Taylor said, leaning down so he was within inches of his face.

"Adams sent some investor down to look at a mining project in Bolivia. It was all a big scam. They were supposed to kill everyone but him, so he would come back to the States financially ruined. Adams'

company loaned him a boatload of cash and they were going to muscle him into helping them launder their drug money when he couldn't
pay them back." He grabbed the side of the dumpster and struggled to
his feet. Blood ran down off his chin and the side of his face. Just as he
got up to a half-standing position, Taylor swept his feet out from under
him, dumping him back on the pavement. "I know, I know, another foul
ball, right?" he moaned.

"Nope. That one just felt good, "Taylor said. "What else?"

"That's it. I swear, that's all I know."

This wasn't Taylor's first time to the dance, and experience led
him to believe that the man had given it up way too easy. Sure, he was
hurting, but not bad enough to roll over so quickly. There had to be
more. He raised his right leg and stomped down with all the force he
could muster, his heel striking squarely on Donaldson's ankle. He felt
bones crunch against concrete like old cookies in a sack.

Donaldson let out another panther scream into the night. Tears
burned in his eyes and he clutched his shattered ankle with both hands.
"What?" he cried out. "What do you want?"

"The rest of the story!" Taylor demanded. "Who was the man
Adams set up?"

"Par...Parker...Gerald Parker." He spat out the name between
coughs of pain. "He sent some moron to take him out, but he blew up
his wife by mistake. I swear, that's it — that's all I know." He rolled over
onto his side, crying into the wet pavement.

"What does this Adams guy know about Chance?"

"Nothing. He just was just some nobody that managed that mining camp down in Bolivia. Adams wanted to get rid of him because he's
a loose end. That's it. I swear." He was to the point that all he could do
was moan through the pain.

Taylor glared down at the broken man. He felt no sympathy for him whatsoever. The ankle he'd crushed was on his left leg. With another anvil-like strike with his heel he smashed his right knee.

Another shriek into the night. Donaldson wretched. He was bleeding, crying, and wallowing in a puddle of his own filth.

Someone must have notified security inside the club because one of the bouncers walked around the side of the building to check things out. "What the hell is going on back here," he hollered.

Taylor turned and gave the intruder a look that let him know he had it handled, and if he didn't want to join the man writhing in agony on the ground, he'd be well advised to let it be.

"Looks like you've got it under control, brother," the bouncer said, shrugging his shoulders. He turned and walked back out of the alley. They paid him to keep peace inside the club. This wasn't his problem, and he damn sure didn't want anything to do with the man who was obviously kicking the hell out of someone who wasn't his concern.

Taylor turned his attention back to Donaldson. "Did your partner know about any of this?"

"What?" He could barely speak and fought to remain conscious.

"Your partner. Did he know?"

"No, he would have killed me if he knew anything about it."

"Good," Taylor said. He turned and walked away from the broken man. He'd call his partner and tell him what he'd confessed to, and where he could find him. He'd let him have the pleasure of scooping the scum up off the pavement and locking his sorry ass up.

Taylor remembered the night he'd sent Agent Donaldson and his partner to bring in Chance for their first meeting. *Guess Chance knocked out the right asshole that first night after all,* he thought. That brought a nice smile to his face.

CHAPTER 50

KNELT carefully on the sloping ridge, about thirty yards above the crude little camp. I was well secluded in the heavy jungle and took my time, studying the activity below, mentally preparing for the next step of my plan.

I'd already slung off the heavy field pack and had it laid on the damp ground beside me. The Beretta 9mm was leathered under my left arm. My holster was unsnapped and ready for a quick draw if needed. I had the Mossberg 12-gauge cradled in the bend of my elbow. There was a double-ought round jacked into the chamber.

I'm a deadly marksman with the pistol but feel and added touch of safety with the scattergun. Good shot or not, the 12-gauge usually finds its target. Just aim in the general direction and fire. Odds are you'll hit something.

I counted about twenty men down below. Some of them slept away the afternoon in crude hammocks. Others lounged around playing cards. A few of them pulled swigs from a bottle they passed among themselves. They were taking life easy, enjoying a little R&R.

I heard something moving through the bush to my right. I resisted the natural instinct of jerking my head around to the sound, knowing that any sudden movement in the jungle can be deadly. It if was a predatory animal, and it hadn't seen me, I didn't want to give away my position.

An icy cold chill ran up my spine and my sixth sense kicked in. This wasn't some random animal. It was a much deadlier predator.

A circle of cold steel pressed against the base of my neck. It felt smaller than a dime in circumference, but that didn't give me any peace of mind. It was more than enough to spit out a bullet that would end my life.

I knew now that the commotion had been a planned distraction to draw my attention away from the man who'd moved up behind me, and who would now decide whether I lived or died.

Three heavily camouflaged men emerged from the bush, each with an assault weapon trained on me. I rose slowly to my feet, the cold steel still pressed hard to the back of my neck, never breaking contact. These were seasoned jungle warriors.

"What is your business here, *rubio*?" the man growled. He spoke in broken English, but well enough for me to clearly understand what he was saying. *Rubio* is the Spanish word for blonde. Besides *gringo*, it's the first thing people around here usually call me. There aren't too many blonde-headed, blue-eyed men running around in the Amazon, so needless to say, I'm a bit of a novelty.

"I would like to speak to your *comandante*. I have something I believe he will be very interested in hearing," I said. The man pushed the barrel of the rifle roughly against my neck. With the mere twist of his finger, it would all be over.

The other three soldiers advanced cautiously. One relieved me of the shotgun. The other reached over and snatched the pistol out of my holster. I felt naked.

The stealth-walker behind me removed the steel from the base of my neck and jammed it hard into my shoulder, spinning me around to face him. "What could you possibly have that would be of interest to our *comandante*? I think it would be much better to just kill you now, and divide your boots and clothing among us," he threatened.

I knew I had to take a stand. These men thrived on *machismo* and would chew me to shreds if they sensed even the slightest hint of fear. I also knew there was a fine line between taking a stand and pissing them off.

"It is your decision," I said, standing tall and facing the man squarely. "Today is as good a day to die as any, but I think your *comandante* will be much happier with what I have to offer, than with you wearing my old boots. Besides, if I am wrong, you can always kill me later."

The guerrilla thought it over for a moment. "You are right, *pendejo*."

He poked me hard in the chest with the barrel of the rifle. I turned and started walking down the steep slope toward their camp.

They hadn't killed me. At least not yet. That was a big hurdle to have gotten over. Now, I could deal face-to-face with their commander. I felt certain I could convince him that my plan would be of great benefit to us both. At least that was what I hoped for — and what I was betting my life on.

• • •

I knew immediately who was in charge. He sat on a stump by a makeshift table and had the aura of authority a man doesn't get from the uniform he wears or how many ribbons decorate his chest. This man had earned his position and the respect of his men and earned it the hard way.

To the untrained eye, their *comandante* might appear worn from too much hard time in the jungle. His clothes were old and tattered, his stringy hair hung long and unkept from under his cap, and his salt-and-pepper beard grew in scraggly patches. But I could see the real story in his eyes. They were bright and clear with determination and purpose.

This man had weathered the storm and was on a mission he was willing to give his life for. That made him one of the deadliest opponents of all.

Setting political and moral standards aside, I respected him for his conviction. As misguided as I might believe his ideology and methods to be, I know there are few who are willing to give it all for what they believe in.

He stabbed a grizzled chunk of meat off the table and raised the heavy blade to his mouth, tearing off a piece like a rabid dog. While he gnawed the meat on one side of his mouth, he spoke out of the other. "What have you brought me, Jorge?"

"Some fine weapons, sir. A good pistol and an excellent scatter-gun." The man was proud of his bounty.

The *comandante* wrestled another piece of tough meat from the tip of his knife, considering their capture. "And the *gringo*? Why is he still alive? I am surprised you are not wearing his boots."

My captor gave me a hard stare.

"I have something that is much more valuable than my old boots," I said.

I'd obviously spoken out of turn and the camp fell silent. All eyes were on me now, waiting to see how their leader would respond.

The seasoned guerrilla took the last bite of meat from the knife and flung the blade violently in my direction, spearing a tree not six inches from my head.

I didn't move, maintaining my stare with the hard man's eyes.

"So, tell me, *gringo*, what is it you have that is so valuable that I should not kill you?" He rolled my shotgun over in his hands, admiring the weapon.

"May I smoke?" I asked. I was trying to appear as nervous as possible.

He nodded his permission, smiling at my discomfort.

I slowly lifted the flap of my shirt pocket, revealing the top of a pack of cigarettes. I nodded toward him for his approval.

"If you wish," he said. "It is likely to be your last." Everyone in camp broke out into roars of laughter at my expense.

Suddenly, the revelry stopped. The sound was replaced by dozens of rifles clattering into place. The men stood serious and silent; their weapons trained on me with deadly intentions. I felt the threatening presence of them all, intent on turning me into a memory.

When I'd reached into my pocket for a cigarette, I slipped out a single shot, nickel-plated .38 derringer, which I now held to the forehead of their leader. The man who'd taught me about surviving in the jungles of the Amazon had told me to always keep the little peacemaker concealed in a pack of cigarettes in my pocket, just in case. At the time, I couldn't imagine I'd ever be in a situation where I'd need it. Now, I was grateful for the sage advice.

"It seems as though the tables have turned," I said calmly.

The *comandante* nodded his head in approval. *This man is worthy of his life, and not a cowering fool in the face of death*, he thought. But he also knew he had to save face in front of his men. "At the snap of my fingers, my men will cut you to ribbons," he declared.

"This is true, but with that same snap of your fingers, you will also follow me into the grave," I said, keeping the derringer steady in my hand, slowly cocking back the hammer. "Who will lead your men to victory, then? The men who allowed me to walk into your camp with this pistol? Is that really who you want to trust with the success of your cause?" I'd given him a way out — a way to save face.

"You are right," he agreed. "This is not the time for us to die." The hardened warrior motioned for his men to lower their weapons. "Sit, and we will discuss this matter you say is of such great importance."

I thumbed down the hammer and laid the small derringer on the table, sliding it over and offering it as a gift. I reached up and yanked the heavy-bladed knife out of the tree. I stabbed a piece of meat and tore it off with my teeth, gnawing at it like a rabid dog, just as he had done.

CHAPTER 51

ALAN Breckenridge slouched in the health club sauna, breathing in the steam and paying the price for what he'd done to his body over the last few days. He had a heavy cotton towel wrapped around his waist and another draped over his head, slowly sweating the poison out of his system. He stared at the front-page headlines on the soggy newspaper in his lap. The world continued to move forward, even though it seemed like his life had come to a screeching halt. He knew it was time to bury his self-pity and fight for what he loved. He'd take a day or two to recuperate, and then get back on track to take back what he'd worked for his entire life. This time he was committed to doing it without the lies and deception.

"Hey, buddy, you mind if I take a look at part of that paper?"

Deep in thought, Breckenridge had been oblivious to anyone else in the sauna. "Sure," he said. He peeled off a few pages and looked up, offering them to the man. He was trying to be polite but had no interest whatsoever to enter into any steam room chit-chat. "Here you go," he said, and then recognized the man. It was Thomas Williamson, president of Southwest Surety Bank.

Not only was Southwest Surety one of the largest banks in the region, but it was also where J. Edward maintained his corporate and personal accounts — at least the ones he kept in-country.

"Alan," Williamson said, surprised. "I didn't realize that was you under the monk hood." He laughed and the heavy jowls shook under his chin. He was at least a hundred pounds overweight, smoked too many cigars, and drank way too much whisky. But he also controlled one of the powerhouse banks in a five-state region.

"Sorry, I was a million miles off in thought," Breckenridge said.

"Hell, that's okay. That's the same thing my wife says when I crawl into bed at night," he laughed. But I am a little surprised to see you here."

"Why are you surprised?"

"I stopped by your office yesterday and they said you were out of the country. Actually, they said they weren't sure if you were coming back at all — something about you taking a position in South America."

So, that's what they're telling people about me, Breckenridge thought. "I just got back last night," he lied.

"That's probably why you look like hell. Jet lag can be a bitch."

"There is something I need to talk to you about, Thomas. Something important."

"No problem. Want me to swing by your office tomorrow?" Williamson was always looking for any excuse he could find to visit the corporate offices of Frontier Financial. The girls were pretty, there was always good whiskey on hand, and J. Edward had a seemingly endless supply of contraband Cuban cigars.

Breckenridge took on an extremely serious attitude. "I think this is something better discussed at your office, and I'd appreciate it if you didn't say anything to J. Edward about it. In fact, it would probably be better if you didn't mention seeing me at all."

Williamson gave him a quizzical look.

"Listen, it's just that I haven't told anybody that I'm back. I'd like to take a day or two to rest up before getting back to the grind. You know how it is."

"Sure, I can understand that. Come on by anytime tomorrow," he said, getting up and slapping a wet palm on Breckenridge's knee.

"Thanks, Thomas. And I'll bring you a box of those cigars you like so much."

"Now, you're talking," Williamson said, waddling out of the room.

Breckenridge knew this would be his first step toward climbing out of the sewer he'd let his life become. He draped the towel back over his head and breathed in another lungful of steam.

CHAPTER 52

DON Taylor sat across from Special Agent Peters in the Oklahoma City offices of the FBI. After he'd dealt with his partner Saturday night, Peters had called and asked him if they could meet.

"I still can't wrap my mind around it. I can't believe he was dirty, and I didn't have the first damn clue," he said, shaking his head. "We were partners for twelve years — like brothers. At least I thought we were." He stared down into a half-empty cup of coffee. Nothing was left but lukewarm mud.

"It's a helluva' thing to try and figure out," Taylor said. "I've seen it more times than I'd like to remember, and I'll never be able to stomach it."

"After you called, I went straight to the alley behind the Stone Horse." He swirled the end of a pencil around in his coffee. He tilted the cup and watched the sludge in the bottom move around like brown river silt. He couldn't bring himself to look Taylor in the eye. "I hardly recognized him lying there by that dumpster. Before I even said a word, he started making excuses, claiming how innocent he was. I knew right then and there that he was just what you said he was." He finally looked up, the pain of betrayal in his eyes. "It made me sick — physically sick. Hell, I puked my guts out right there in that alley like some piss-ant rookie at his first homicide." He shook his head, embarrassed.

Taylor stayed quiet. He knew it was best to let him get it off his chest.

"I wanted to kill him. Eighteen years on the job and always by the book and I wanted to put a bullet in his skull." He went back to stirring the pencil around in his cup.

"Peters!" Taylor snapped. He wanted the man's full attention.

Peters looked up.

"You wanted to, but you didn't. That's what's important," Taylor reassured him. "Still by the book. You scooped him up and dropped him in the hole where he belongs, and by God, you'll be there when they send him away for good."

"Yeah, I guess you're right."

"He'll get what he's got coming, and I promise, it will be a lot worse than you putting a bullet in his head."

Peters nodded. He was looking at Taylor, but still in a mental fog.

"What can I do for you now?" Taylor asked. "You said you wanted to talk, and I'm sure it wasn't about how much of a piece of shit your old partner is."

Agent Peters' face took back the hard edge of a determined cop. He was a good man behind his badge. "I want you to help me burn the bastards he was working with," he said, with fierce conviction in his voice. "I want to bring them down and bring them down hard. I know you can move in places where I can't, and I want to take advantage of that."

"Now, you're talking," Taylor said, smiling.

CHAPTER 53

GERALD Parker sat on the couch in his living room. The windows were still boarded over because the explosion that killed his wife had blown out all the glass. At the moment, he preferred the darkness.

His daughters were still with his folks. He didn't think it would be a good idea to bring them back here this soon, if ever.

There was bright yellow crime scene tape wrapped around the front yard. The grass was scorched and there was a huge black mark burned into the street from the explosion. Parker wanted to see the reminders of it all. He wanted the brutality to hit him square in the face and prepare him for what he knew he had to do.

Gerald Parker had never been a big fan of guns, but this was different. The little .25 caliber pistol he held in his hand gave him an odd comfort. A friend had given it to him several years ago, saying it would be good to keep in his car when he was out on construction sites late at night. He'd never even fired it. It had been in the original box in the top of his closet ever since the day he'd gotten it. Right now, it felt damn good in his hands.

They'll pay for what they've done. As sure as I'm a man, they'll pay, he thought, rolling the little automatic over and over in his palm. This was the first time he'd handled a gun since that .357 magnum down in Bolivia. But that was just for show. He had a purpose for this this weapon. A deadly purpose.

CHAPTER 54

THE offer I'd made to the small band of guerrillas worked. I'd appealed to their politics and greed. It was a combination that was more than they could resist. I'd told them that a Bolivian military officer was operating a cocaine production facility less than a kilometer across the border into Peru. I further explained that they brought most of their workers over from Bolivia, except for a few local laborers, who they only paid a pittance of a salary and treated like slaves. I also told them that the finished product would be smuggled through Colombia and into the United States, and that their motherland and cause wouldn't benefit one red cent from the millions of dollars being made.

"They are spitting in the faces of our people!" the *comandante* yelled.

I could see that the more he thought about the situation, the more he despised what was happening. I'd planted the seed. Now, all I had to do was let rage and jealousy nourish it.

"We shall destroy these pigs and feed the soil of our land with their blood!" He thrust his rifle high into the air, rallying his troops with his fierce rebel call. The entire camp broke out into a riot of screams and cheers, everyone pumping their weapons high above their heads, supporting their leader's call to action.

I knew now that I had the help I'd hoped for. I wondered what Don Taylor would think when he found out I was aligning myself with a band of communist guerillas.

"What shall come of the profits we take from these capitalist swine?" the *comandante* asked.

"You and your men can seize whatever equipment and drugs we find to fund your cause."

"And you? What is it that you want?" he asked.

"Colonel Zoto. I want him alive."

"Then you shall have him," he said.

I stood up from the table, extending my hand to the man. He took it in a strong grip, sealing our bond.

"We will leave at sunrise. Tonight, make yourself comfortable in our camp."

I picked up my pack and holstered the Beretta. He handed me the shotgun and slipped the small derringer into his pocket.

"*Gracias*," I said, and walked over to find a spot to bed down for the night, right in the middle of a camp full of killers. The *Sendero Luminoso*. My new partners.

CHAPTER 55

LISA Dalton knew she'd been away long enough. It was time to get back to her life, even if it was going to be without Alan. She had called her office earlier to see how things were going and to let them know that she'd be back the day after tomorrow. As far as they knew, she was on the vacation she'd been bragging about taking with Alan when he got back from Bolivia. She had already decided to go back to the condo, pack her things, and check into a hotel while she looked for a new place to live.

Although she'd thoroughly enjoyed spending a few days at home, she knew she hadn't been the best of company. Her mother continually questioned her about why she wasn't her usual self, and Lisa kept telling her she thought she was coming down with a cold or something. She couldn't bring herself to tell her about all of the horrible things she'd found out about Alan, and that the relationship she'd been so proud of, was now in shambles. Her mother loved Alan, and even depended on him for advice about her personal financial affairs. He'd always been such a great help with so much of what Lisa's father had handled before his death. Lisa knew her mother would be heartbroken when she found out they wouldn't be getting married. She wasn't ready to deal with that yet, so she'd explained that he was out of the country on business, and that she just felt like coming home for a few days.

Lisa stood in her childhood bedroom in the third-floor walkup apartment in the Mission District of San Francisco. The window was open and there were the familiar noises of the city coming up from the street — the laughter of children playing on the sidewalk, the singsong call of vendors selling fruit from the small stand on the corner, and the sounds of church bells ringing in the distance from one of the old missions. She felt safe here.

A cool breeze billowed her curtains back into the room. She stood next to her bed and finished packing, wondering what she was going to do if Alan was at the condo when she got there. She prayed that he wouldn't be. The last thing she wanted was to have to face him. Even though they'd had several amazing years together, the only thoughts she had of him now were what she'd seen in those police photos, and of all the horrible things those crime reports said that he'd done.

She zipped her suitcase closed and looked around one last time at the mementos from her childhood. Her room looked just like it did the day she moved out to go to college.

"Lisa, are you okay in there?" Her mother gently rapped on the door.

"Yeah, Mom, I'm fine," she lied.

She plopped down on the soft bed, sinking deep into the thick comforter. She rolled over onto a pile of lace-lined pillows and hugged her old stuffed bear. She'd have one more good cry, and then leave for the airport, and back to her broken life.

CHAPTER 56

ALAN Breckenridge sat at the conference table in Thomas Williamson's office. A secretary brought them coffee on a silver tray. There was a hand-painted blue and white china pot, cream, sugar, two delicate china cups, two saucers, and two silver spoons. She sat it all on the table and then carefully poured them a cup of the steaming brew.

Williamson waited for the door to close behind her, and then slipped a pint of whisky out of his bottom desk drawer. He tilted the tip of the bottle toward Breckenridge, offering him a shot. He declined. Williamson splashed some into his own coffee. Breckenridge didn't know if he would ever be able to tolerate liquor again after saturating his body for so many consecutive days.

As usual, there was the endless casual conversation about the weather, the economy, family, and all the other nonsense nobody really cared about, but always felt obligated to tolerate prior to any real business being discussed.

Williamson took a sip from the spiked coffee and picked up one of the expensive cigars that Breckenridge had brought him. He rolled it between his thumb and forefinger, and then clipped off the end. He turned the barrel slowly in the flame of his gold lighter before sticking it in his mouth. He puffed slowly, making a grand ceremony of how he fired it up. "Damn fine cigar, Alan." He leaned back in his chair, looking toward the ceiling like he was admiring the blue-gray smoke. "Now, what is it that you wanted to talk to me about?"

Breckenridge opened his briefcase and took out a small stack of folders. He slid them across the polished surface of the desk. "Drug money, Thomas, and just how much of it you have in your bank," he said flatly.

Williamson coughed out two hard puffs of smoke and rocked his chair forward, planting his feet hard on the floor and slapping his hands flat on the desk. "What in the hell are you talking about?" He slurped the last of his coffee in one huge gulp, and then banged the china cup onto the saucer. Delicate and dainty just left the room. He was panic-stricken. Being caught laundering drug money would destroy his bank, as well as everything else he'd spent a lifetime building. He looked down at the files like they were radioactive, afraid to touch them.

"Actually, the money isn't in your bank just yet, but it will be shortly." Breckenridge took a slow sip of coffee, allowing the moment of suspense to play out." J. Edward made a ten-million-dollar transfer a while back. The documents you have in front of you are proof that it was used as a down payment for a multi-million-dollar shipment of cocaine that will be arriving in the next few weeks."

Williamson forwent the cup and took a hard swig straight from the bottle.

"The profits from the sale of those drugs will be laundered through various Frontier Federal operations, and then run through your bank. I know because I'm the one who set it all up."

"Why are you telling me this?" Williamson asked. He began to sweat profusely.

"Because now that you know about it, if you don't report it, you'll lose it all. Your business, your reputation. You can watch it all go swirling down the drain."

"Holy shit, man! I don't have anything to do with any of this."

"I know, Thomas. You've always been straight with me, so I'm warning you in advance. Do something about it or suffer the consequences."

Williamson started breathing in short gasps like he was having a hard time catching his breath.

"I'm going to bring J. Edward down, and you're going to help me, or you'll go down with him. It's as simple as that."

"Of course, I'll help," he said. "What do you want me to do?"

"Contact the authorities. The FBI, State Banking Commission, DEA, Federal Reserve, IRS, Homeland Security — call them all. They'll put a freeze on J. Edwards accounts while they investigate, and he'll get a financial colonoscopy like he can't even imagine."

"Absolutely. I'll get right on it," Williams promised. "We can't have this kind of thing in our bank — we just can't." The liquor hadn't done much to settle his nerves.

"I'll give you a call in a couple of days to see how things are going." Breckenridge snapped his briefcase closed, leaving the toxic files spread out on the table when he left.

CHAPTER 57

DON Taylor lounged in a dark corner of the hospital room. The only light was the red and green glow coming from the monitors hooked up to the patient. An IV bottle hung over the bed, suspended from a slim chrome tube, and there was a clear plastic line dripping liquid into the man's arm. His wrists were handcuffed to the railing. One of his legs was suspended by a network of wires hanging from a special orthopedic framework, and the other rested on a stack of pillows. Both were wrapped in heavy plaster casts. His face was a mess of puffy bruises and contusions, stitched and stapled shut. His condition wasn't life-threatening, but it was debilitating, and very painful.

"How's your love life, stud?" Taylor whispered into the silence of the room

"What?" The man was groggy from all the medication and didn't recognize the voice.

"It's me, your party buddy," Taylor said, stepping closer and clicking on the bedside lamp.

"What do you...how did you...," he said, panicked. He jerked his bound wrists, rattling the steel cuffs against the bed railing, wishing he could somehow escape. No such luck.

Before he could say anything else, Taylor clamped his left hand over his mouth. With his right hand he flicked open a switchblade, pressing the razor-sharp edge of the knife to his throat. He wanted to be certain he understood just how serious things were about to get. "Just be calm, pal. I didn't get all I needed the other night. Behave yourself and I won't have to bleed you out. Understand?" Former FBI Agent Donaldson was terrified, shaking his head in agreement.

Taylor released his hand from his mouth. "I want you to tell me more about this Adams guy — his routine, his likes, dislikes, who he trusts, and so on. I want to know everything you know about the man."

Donaldson had no intention of even pretending like he was going to resist. He'd already experienced firsthand how brutal Taylor could be, and now that the cat was out of the bag, he hoped everything he did might help trim a little time off the prison sentence he knew was coming. He had nothing to lose, so he began spilling his guts.

Taylor kept the knife pressed to his throat.

CHAPTER 58

I KNELT next to the *comandante* in the heavy undergrowth, assessing what lay before us. Combat butterflies stirred in both of our stomachs. He was a seasoned veteran with years of experience in raids like this. This was only my second time entering such an arena. The first time was during the attack on our camp back on Rio Solocama. Now, we shared the same anxieties. When the bullets start flying and adrenaline takes over, there's no time for fear or reflection. Those are things to be had before, and then again after. This was the time to consider what lay before us, and to think about our impending fight for life.

The adrenaline wouldn't really kick in until after the first shots rang out, and any man who brags that he has no apprehensions about entering into a fight for his life, is either a liar, or crazy. Neither makes for a good comrade in arms.

I thought about the drastic contrast in beliefs that I had with these men. They were radical communists who stood against everything I held dear — godless men who scoffed at Christian values and openly berated the country I loved. But now, huddled together in the thick cover of jungle, I could sense their fears — thoughts of family and loved ones and whether they would ever see them again. Strip away the layers of politics and hatred, and maybe we weren't so different after all. Just men doing a job we knew had to be done.

The *comandante* raised his fist and swirled it in an imaginary circle above his head. His men saw the signal and disappeared into the jungle, taking their positions around the facility below. Although they might look crude and unorganized at first glance, they knew what had to be done, and were ready to give their lives if necessary.

The *comandante* had devised a plan for attack that assigned each man a position in the perimeter. When the shooting began, they could maximize coverage and damage while minimizing the risk of hitting each other in their own crossfire. Their leader and I planned on going in together, right down the middle. We would draw attention to ourselves and away from the surrounding marauders.

I glanced at my watch. Five minutes to go. The second hand seemed to crawl from one hash mark to the next.

I drew my pistol and worked back the action, confirming that it was loaded, and slipped it back into the holster. Then, I gripped the shotgun. I had eight double-ought rounds fed into the extended magazine and one jacked into the chamber.

I looked over at my *compadre* in arms. No words were needed. We nodded to each other. We were ready.

I glanced at my watch again. The fuse was lit and there were three minutes to burn.

CHAPTER 59

GERALD Parker flipped through the magazines in the hotel gift shop, trying to find something to take his mind off what he'd come to do. The selection wasn't too interesting. He could care less who was humping who these days, or if Kim Kardashian's after-baby ass looked bigger than usual in her latest bikini-clad romp on the beach. He was getting restless. He'd sat out by the pool for a while, but watching families laughing and enjoying each other brought back too many painful memories of times he and Janet had spent with their girls. He knew he'd never have that again. He'd tried sitting in his room watching television, but the selection of shows wasn't much better than what the magazines had to offer, and he felt the walls starting to close in around him.

He looked over at a shelf stacked with stuffed animals, T-shirts, snow globes, and all the other tourist crap he'd seen in every other hotel he'd ever been in. But then, right there in the middle of all that useless souvenir clutter he saw one of those old-fashioned monkeys that clanged two small cymbals together when you wound it up. He remembered having one just like it when he was a kid.

He walked over to the cashier to pay for a bottle of water and a bag of chips.

"Will that be all?" the cashier asked.

"Yeah, that's it."

Then, he looked back over at the mechanical monkey.

"Wait a second."

He walked over and picked up the toy and laid it on the counter.

"I'll take this, too," he said.

"Oh, I bet your kids will love it," she said.

Gerald Parker smiled. It was the first time he'd smiled since the explosion that blew up his wife.

CHAPTER 60

ALAN Breckenridge caught an early flight from Oklahoma City to Phoenix. He changed planes in Dallas, and then again in San Antonio. When he arrived, he went straight to his hotel to shower, shave, and put on a fresh suit. He wanted to look his best for his appointment.

Now, the man's wife greeted him at the front door of their home, and just like every other time he'd seen her, every hair was in place and her makeup was perfect. She wore a simple floral print housedress, and on her, it looked elegant.

Breckenridge was surprised that she remembered him since it had been so many years since they'd last seen each other. She invited him in, leading him to an enclosed sun porch at the back of the house, and then set out a platter of fresh fruit.

"Mr. Breckenridge, would you like something to drink? Maybe some lemonade?" she asked.

"No, ma'am, but thank you. And please, call me Alan."

"Aren't you sweet," she said.

There was an apricot poodle that scurried over and started sniffing at his shoes.

"Precious, get away from there." She reached down and scooped the little dog up in her arms. "I'm sorry, Alan. We don't get too many visitors these days."

"That's okay. He probably smelled my dog," he lied. He and Lisa had talked about getting a puppy, but never had. He'd just said it to make the woman feel less embarrassed.

"My husband shouldn't be much longer," she said, and walked out of the room, carrying her lapdog with her.

Breckenridge wore a dark gray pinstriped suit. He had on a crisp white shirt with a button-down collar and a solid maroon tie. He'd forgone his usual blow-dried hairstyle and combed through some gel to emphasize the razor-sharp part. His shoes were shined to a perfect sheen and his nails were neat and trim from the manicure he'd gotten the day before. Ultra-conservative was the style for the day.

Breckenridge held the man he'd come to see in high regard. He was from a different era, and he respected him immensely. This was the first time he'd been to his home in Arizona. The last time they'd met had been several years ago in New York City, where the family organization was headquartered. The man had moved to Phoenix to semi-retire and enjoy the dry, warm climate in his declining years. But anyone who believed he was out of the business completely was making a deadly mistake. He still called the shots, but in much less obvious ways.

The old gentleman walked into the room, taking each step cautiously. He wore off-white chino slacks and a dark blue silk shirt that hung loose outside of his pants. He had on a pair of light blue deck shoes and his gray hair was thick and combed neatly. His dark eyes were surprisingly bright and alert in contrast to his aging body.

Breckenridge stood, waiting patiently for him to make it across the room.

"Alan, it's good to see you," he said, nearing the couch.

"You too, sir," Breckenridge said, extending his hand.

Although he walked with an aged gait, the man still had an impressive grip. He sat down and motioned for Breckenridge to do the same. Then, he reached over and took a slice of mango off the platter his wife had left on the table.

"*Don* Vicente, I appreciate you taking the time to see me," Breckenridge began.

The man nodded. Vicente Toscalini might be in his eighties, but he still wielded considerable influence across the country. He had been the right-hand man and lifelong confidant to J. Edward's father, and assumed his role as head of the organization when he died. It was the position that J. Edward believed he rightly deserved.

The family business maintained their empire on the foundation it had been built upon decades ago — contraband goods, loan sharking, gambling, and murder for hire. They believed in sticking to the basics, and absolutely abhorred the rise of the drug trade. Despite their ruthless and deadly dealings, these were old school men who believed drugs to be an unforgivable scourge on families.

J. Edward had gone berserk when he'd learned that he wasn't going to be given his father's role in the organization, and the others had wanted him eliminated. It was Vicente Toscalini who vouched for him, promising to keep him in line and out of their way.

Toscalini knew that J. Edward's father had never wanted his son to be in the family business. He had even legally changed the boy's name before he reached his teenage years. He knew the family name would be a burden to his success in the legitimate business world and made the difficult sacrifice for his only son. It broke his heart, knowing that if he ever had any grandchildren, they wouldn't carry his name, but he did what he believed was best for J. Edward's future.

"Alan, when you called you said there was some matter of grave concern for our business," Toscalini said.

"It's about J. Edward."

The old man held up his hand, signaling for Breckenridge to stop. "J. Edward chose his own path after his father died. I know he was hurt when he wasn't called upon to take the position that I was given, but we knew he wasn't ready for the responsibility. He was too reckless and impulsive," he said.

Breckenridge sat quietly, taking in the man's words.

"Out of respect for his father, we gave him a very profitable enterprise to oversee in Oklahoma, but as far as we're concerned, he has no more involvement with our business."

"I understand," Breckenridge said.

"You made the choice to go with him instead of staying and working with us in New York. If you're having problems with him now, I'm sorry, but you know once that door is closed, it cannot be reopened." He turned his hands over, showing his palms and giving Breckenridge the opportunity to speak.

"I realize that I'm the one who made the decision to leave New York, and I'm the one who has to live with that choice. But I still hold tremendous respect for you and the others, and I don't want to see any unnecessary trouble come your way because of the mistakes I believe J. Edward is making now." Breckenridge was trying to be as diplomatic as possible. He was also trying to be vague, and still convey to Toscalini that J. Edward's ship was about to hit the rocks. He knew if he went into too much detail the old man would see him as being disloyal to J. Edward. To a man like Vicente Toscalini, disloyalty was a sin punishable by death.

What Toscalini didn't know, was that J. Edward had blackmailed Breckenridge into going to Oklahoma with him. Breckenridge could only hope that he would take his ambiguous warning and investigate matters on his own.

"I understand, Alan, and I appreciate you bringing this to my attention." Toscalini stood up from his chair. "Feel free to call on me anytime."

"Thank you, *don* Vicente," Breckenridge said. He knew his offer to call on him meant he did in fact appreciate the way he'd handled the matter. He also knew the moment he left, the old man would be on the phone to his minions, having them dig into whatever J. Edward was up to.

Bottom line: Breckenridge had accomplished his mission.

CHAPTER 61

THE condo felt foreign. It didn't feel like it had ever been the happy home she'd once shared with Alan. Now, it was clean and orderly, with an almost sterile atmosphere. Everything was in its place, unlike the disarray she'd fled from not that many nights ago. But Lisa knew it wasn't the same. Her closets were empty, and by the time she left there today, she would remove every reminder that she'd ever lived there at all.

There was a dull ache in her heart as she packed the last few knick-knacks — all the things that reminded her of family and of the places she and Alan had been together. There was an old black-and-white photo of her father when he was in the Navy, and a picture of her and her parents when she was a baby, with her dad holding her up on the hood of their red Camaro. There was a shot of her and Alan on their first snorkeling trip to Cozumel, set in a frame surrounded by seashells and sand dollars. So many happy reminders of the past.

List hurt inside, because despite it all, she still loved Alan. She hated him for the lies and deception, but carried him deep in her heart, and she knew that would never change. She shook her head in disbelief, knowing that there really was no logic in love.

CHAPTER 62

D ON Taylor sat at the small breakfast nook in the home of Agent Peters. It was a neat three-bedroom frame house with a detached garage, located in an older suburban neighborhood on the south side of Oklahoma City. Most of the neighbors were retirees who kept their houses and yards neat and well maintained. It was a homey atmosphere where Peters and his wife were comfortable raising their two sons.

"Would you care for some more iced tea, Mr. Taylor?" Peters' wife offered.

"No, thank you," he said. He thought that if he'd chosen a different path in life, this might be what he would have wanted. But he hadn't, and there was business to take care of, so he pushed those silly thoughts out of his mind.

Peter's wife leaned over and kissed her husband on the top of his head. "A woman knows when it's time to let the boys talk shop," she said, sitting the pitcher of iced tea on the counter, and then walking out of the room.

"Thanks, doll," Peters said.

Taylor waited until she'd left the kitchen, and then opened the file he'd brought with him. "Here's what I've got on this Adams guy." He spread the papers out on the Formica tabletop.

"It didn't take long for you to come up with all of this," Peters said, obviously impressed as he perused the material. "Even with the Bureau's resources, it would have taken me weeks to dig up this much information."

"Like you said, I can move in places you can't, and that gives me some quick access to intel." Taylor tipped his glass to his lips, rattling the ice and coaxing out one last sip of the sweet tea.

Peters noticed something interesting and began tapping his finger on the page. "So, that's the connection," he said.

"Yep, none other than the son of Benedetto Marchese, former head of one of the oldest and most powerful crime families of their day."

"Of their day? Hell, man, they've still got a lot of play," Peters said.

"That's what they tell me, but it's not like it used to be."

"Nevertheless, they're still a formidable target for the Bureau."

"J. Edward's birth name was Eduardo Marchese. His old man had his name changed and let his mother raise him in Europe after they separated. It was an unusual thing for an old mobster to do, but he was trying to give the kid a better shot at a legitimate life, and he had the money and connections to get it done. J. Edward was just too damn stupid to take advantage of it. He gravitated back to the family business after his old man died, but the organization did all they could to keep him at arm's length," Taylor explained.

"I thought those boys stayed out of the drug business," Peters said, looking up from the stack of documents.

"That's one of the reasons they didn't want anything to do with J. Edward. Before they sent him here to Oklahoma, he tried his hand in the heroin business back in New York. When they found out, a few of the old guard hauled his ass out to an abandoned warehouse and popped a .22 round into his knee. Just a little motivation for him to clean up his act."

"No kidding?" Peters said.

"That's when Vicente Toscalini vouched for him. His commitment to J. Edward's father to keep an eye on him was the only reason they didn't put a slug in his head"

Taylor reached over and flipped open another file.

Agent Peters studied its contents for a moment.

"Who's this guy?" he asked.

"Alan Breckenridge. He's J. Edward's right-hand man. At least he was. He's sort of dropped off the radar."

"Name doesn't ring a bell," Peters said.

"That's because his real name is Terry Mancini. He was an enforcer for the family back in New York until he got indicted for murder.

"Geez, what a mess," Peters said, looking at the same crime scene photos Lisa Dalton had seen.

"Breckenridge — or Mancini back then, was tasked to take out some rivals that were trying to move in on their territory. Problem was, he got some bad intel and wiped out an entire family by mistake. The wrong family. Mom, dad, kids — he killed them all. And as you can see, he wasn't very delicate in the way he went about it."

"That's an understatement," Peters said, pouring over the gruesome photos. "This is some brutal shit."

"Word is that he caught them in their sleep. Dragged the whole family into one room. Popped the kids first, right in front of their parents. Hell, he even decapitated the dog."

"How'd he keep the needle out of his arm for that one?" Peters asked.

Taylor shuffled through the papers until he came to a particular set of black and white photos. "This first one is what he *used* to look like, and the second one is what he looks like now. They spirited him out of the country before NYPD could lock him down. A nip here and a tuck there, and Terry Mancini became Alan Breckenridge."

"Incredible," Peters said, holding up the two photos, looking for subtle similarities.

"For the last few years, he's been living the good life right here in your own backyard, working for J. Edward Adams III."

"Seems like a habit for these guys to take out innocent bystanders," Peters said, thinking about Gerald Parker's wife being blown up.

"They definitely need to be taken off the count," Taylor declared.

CHAPTER 63

THE *comandante* rose from kneeling to a bent-knee linebacker stance and began shuffling down the steep hillside toward the production facility. I was three meters to his left, moving in the same direction. We both held our weapons at the ready. As we came to within twenty meters of the operation, one of the perimeter sentries spotted our approach and raised his rifle. His reaction was too late. The *comandante* spat out a three-round burst from his AK-47, cutting him down in his tracks. Now, we had everyone's attention and men began swarming toward us.

I raised the Mossberg and racked-off a 12-gauge blast square into the chest of the first advancing defender. It knocked him off his feet like a rampaging guard dog hitting the end of his chain. At the same time the guerrillas sprayed automatic fire into camp from around the perimeter.

A group of about thirty men ran toward us, and then scattered in confusion. Some ran left, some right, and others backpedaled, all returning fire toward attackers they couldn't see in the thick jungle. A few dedicated souls stood their ground with little success. It became obvious that Colonel Zoto had not recruited his men from the trained ranks of the military. These were simple villagers who had been forced into service, issued camouflage clothing and weapons, and expected to defend the operation, even though they had no formal combat training.

The *comandante* laid out figure eights of automatic fire while I pumped off a steady barrage of double-ought rounds from the shotgun.

The camp laborers dropped to their knees, raising their hands high above their heads in surrender. They were unarmed and hadn't signed on for this kind of trouble. The invading guerrillas tried not to hit them, knowing they weren't their primary targets. Besides, they knew they might be able to recruit them into their ranks after the raid was over. If not, they could always kill them later.

The guerrillas continued advancing through camp, closing their circle of attack and finishing off any remaining defenders with deadly bursts of automatic fire. I worked my way around the edge of the installation, kicking in one door after the other in search of Colonel Zoto. I'd seen a small helicopter at the edge of camp, so I knew he was still here.

I laid down the empty shotgun and drew my pistol, sprinting the short distance to the last unchecked building. I slammed my back against the side of the wooden structure, molding myself to the outside wall. I waited for a moment, listening for any sounds coming from inside.

The firing around camp stopped and I assumed the guerrillas had complete control. I looked up and saw the *comandante* and two of his men coming my way. I held out a flat palm, signaling for them to hold their positions. I wanted to check out the building alone. I was concerned that if Colonel Zoto was inside, and began firing, the guerrillas might forget about our deal and kill him before I had the chance to extract the information that I needed.

I caught something out of the corner of my eye in the center of the compound. There was young woman tied to a tree. She'd been gut-shot. The front of her dress was soaked with dark red blood and she was obviously dead. *Looks like Zoto has been up to his old motivational methods*, I thought.

I stepped back and delivered a solid kick to the door. As soon as it burst open Zoto began firing. I took cover and yelled, "Drop your weapon!"

Colonel Zoto quickly wrapped his arm around the throat of Enrique, his camp manager, using him as a human shield. He swung around to face me head-on, pressing his pistol to the man's head. If he thought that might be any kind of deterrent, he was wrong.

I triggered off two 9mm rounds that tore into the hostage's chest, taking care of that problem. Now, he was nothing more than dead weight in Zoto's arms, so he dumped him onto the floor. I took aim and shot Zoto in the shoulder. He dropped his pistol and fell hard to the ground, grabbing at his wound.

I moved in quickly, kicking the weapon away from Zoto's hand and glaring down at the man who'd cast the shadow of death on so many innocent lives.

"*Diablos!*" Who in the hell are you?" he asked.

"I'm the man who gave Ramiro Dueñas his final birthday present."

"You!" he screamed.

I ground the toe of my boot into his raw wound. He howled in pain.

"You're going to tell me who your partner is in the States, or I'll turn you over to the guerrillas," I threatened.

"I will tell you nothing!" he said defiantly, spitting at me, and then reaching down and grabbing a fragment grenade he had clipped to his belt. He jerked the pin out with his teeth, releasing the handle and activating the short timer.

I spun around and sprinted for the door, yelling for the *comandante* and his men to get back.

I'd already covered a lot of territory but kept running. The first blast was minor, but I knew the next shock was going to be rough. A split-second later the ground rumbled, and the building erupted into a thunderous ball of flames. The concussion of the blast slammed me to the ground and the *comandante* and his men were knocked off their feet.

The building where I'd found Colonel Zoto had been the main storage facility for dozens of fifty-five-gallon drums of fuel. I'd also seen a mountain of cocaine that was packed in hard brown packets, ready for shipment.

The blast solved the problem of how I was going to keep the guerrillas from getting their hands on the drugs. No matter what kind of deal we'd made, I knew I could never let that happen. Unfortunately, the explosion also consumed the life and body of Colonel Juan Zoto, and along with him, the critical information that I was after.

"I am sorry you did not get the colonel alive," the *comandante* said, moving up next to me.

"And I'm sorry you didn't get the drugs you needed to help fund your cause. They were in that building," I said, pointing toward the raging fire.

"It is alright," he said, a sly grin creeping across his face. "We have found much cash and many weapons, and there is plenty of food I can use to feed my men. We are well satisfied with our take here today."

"I'm glad," I said. "And thank you for your help."

The *comandante* took on a sudden and unexpected change of personality, reverting to the hardened communist guerrilla who despised all capitalistic *norteamericanos*. "We did this for *our* cause — not for your benefit. Now, it is over, and I would suggest that you go on your way. It will be best that we never meet again," he threatened.

The band of guerrillas circled us. Their dull-eyed expressions suggested that at the snap of their leader's fingers they would kill me faster than they could squash a cockroach under boot, and with about as much remorse.

I didn't know if this was all part of some grand show of *machismo* that the *comandante* was putting on for his men, or if he was serious. But either way, I understood it was time for me to move on.

I didn't offer him my hand because I knew there was no way in hell that he could ever accept it in front of his men, especially after what he'd just said.

"*Gracias,*" I said, quietly under my breath.

"*Por nada* — thank you," he whispered, as I walked past him.

CHAPTER 64

THOMAS Williamson slumped in a chair in J. Edward's office. As much as he usually enjoyed his visits there, this was one he wished he didn't have to make.

"Damnit, J. Edward! That crazy bastard could ruin us all," he said "Hell, man, he could cause me to lose my bank and everything else that I've worked my entire life to build. He's got it all — copies of transactions, correspondence, our contacts with foreign banks, the whole stinking ball of wax." Williamson was obviously shaken by Breckenridge's visit to his office.

"Do not worry about it, Thomas. I will handle it," J. Edward said. It constantly amazed him how men could crumble so easily under a little pressure, and Thomas Williamson was a weak man crumbling fast.

"Handle it?" How in the hell are you going to handle it?" His hands were shaking so badly he couldn't get his drink up to his lips. He'd passed on the offer of a cigar, but there was no way in hell he'd pass on a stiff shot.

"Do you know if Breckenridge has spoken to anyone else about this"

"Not yet. He wants me to take it to the authorities," Williamson said.

"With good reason. I am sure he is worried they might dig a little too deep into his own background if he is the one that makes the initial contact," J. Edward said.

"I don't know what you're talking about, and I don't want to know. All I want to hear is that you're going to clean this mess up," Williamson grumbled.

"Stop sniveling!" J. Edward was beginning to feel like he was dealing with a whining child.

Williamson sat up straight. He most certainly wasn't used to being talked to like that.

"When Breckenridge calls, tell him that the investigators from the State Banking Commission want to speak with him in person. Say that they are interested in hearing his side of the story but need more details. Tell him they want to meet at one of those cheap motels over off Highway 66 on the north side of town because they are taking every precaution to protect his identity. He will believe that. Have someone rent a room. Use a fake name and pay for it with cash. Drop the key off at the office with a note detailing the time and place, and then forget about it."

"What are you going to do?" Williamson asked.

"What part of 'forget about it' did you not understand," J. Edward snapped. "I said forget about it, and that is exactly what I meant."

"Whatever you say. I don't want to know anything else about this mess. I agreed to help you launder that cash, but that was supposed to be the end of it for me. The rest of this mess is *your* problem." Williamson hoisted himself up, drained his drink, and headed for the door.

"Thomas."

Williamson stopped and looked back.

"You *are* involved, and you will burn with the rest of us if this goes unresolved," J. Edward said in a menacing tone.

CHAPTER 65

ALAN Breckenridge sat and listened to the line ring at the other end of the call. His palms were sweating, and he felt light-headed and short of breath. Of all his exploits, this was the first time he'd ever felt so physically anxious.

"Bluewater Associates," said the perky voice.

"Lisa Dalton, please." His voice was shaky.

"One moment," the woman said, putting him on hold.

Breckenridge waited, listening to music on the line for what seemed like an eternity.

"Lisa Dalton. How may I help you?"

Hearing her say even those few words was like a miracle. Only a few days ago he believed he'd never hear her voice again. He felt a heavy lump in his throat.

"Hello? This is Lisa Dalton. How may I help you?" she said again.

"Lisa," he said.

She immediately recognized his voice and was suddenly filled with a flood of emotions. She felt all the anger, the hate, and the hurt of his deception. Mixed in with it all she felt the love she still had for him.

Breckenridge summoned his strength. "Lisa, I know you're hurt and angry, and probably never wanted to hear from me again, but I would at least like the opportunity to try and explain why I did what I did, and why I couldn't tell you the truth."

She remained silent, tears welling up in her eyes.

"Is there any chance that we could meet? Just to talk. Please." He knew he was begging and didn't feel the least bit ashamed.

"I'll think about it," she said, and hung up.

She'd rehearsed this moment a thousand times in her mind, ever since she'd seen those gruesome crime scene photos and police reports — what she'd say to him if he ever had the nerve to contact her again. Now, that the moment was here, she couldn't do it. She knew she could never hate the only man she'd ever truly loved.

All she felt like she could do now was to cry. After a minute, she gathered her emotions, picked up her cellphone, and tapped out the message.

Starbucks. 6:00 tomorrow evening.

She was going to let him try and explain it to her. Try to justify why he'd broken her heart — crushed her dreams.

CHAPTER 66

MADE my way into Pata just before sundown. It's a picturesque little village set high on the side of a mountain overlooking the Rio Tuichi Valley. I'd left the band of guerrillas and the charred remains of the cocaine facility almost thirty-six hours behind me. Moving through the jungle was a slow, tedious process, but I wanted to put as much distance as I could between me and that location. Traveling through the bush at night was especially dangerous, but being found by any military patrols searching for the man they believed killed Colonel Zoto was an even greater risk.

Mental and physical strain was taking a hard toll. I'd been living on catnaps and resting whenever I could, but I'd finally hit the end of my physical reserves and seriously needed some rest.

As the crow flies, I hadn't traveled very far, but I was confident that the distance and the imposing terrain I'd put between me and the carnage I'd left behind was enough.

I stood at the far edge of the little village, doing a cursory recon and waiting for any locals to appear. Letting them make first contact would arouse less suspicion.

There were a handful of white-washed adobe huts with thatched roofs, all built around the small village square, and an old adobe church with a crumbling bell tower. It was dead silence. Not even a dog barked, so I knew if there was life nearby, they were huddled up in their huts, checking me out. That also meant that there were probably dozens of curious eyes on me right now, peeking through darkened doorways and waiting for their designated ambassador to venture out and confront the stranger.

Within a few minutes, a haggard old man walked out of his hut.

"*Buenos dias*," I said. I had the 12-gauge slung casually over my shoulder by the strap with the barrel pointed down. My pistol was holstered under my bush jacket and out of sight. I was trying to appear as unthreatening as possible.

The man met me in the middle of the clearing and offered a calloused hand in greeting. He appeared permanently bent over, probably from too many years of doing work intended for mules.

I shook his hand carefully, and as soon as he began to speak, I realized that I had a new obstacle to overcome. I couldn't tell if he was speaking Quechua, or Aymara, but I knew it was one of the indigenous languages that I didn't understand. I tried a few phrases in Spanish, but I might as well have been speaking Chinese. We just stood there, smiling and nodding to each other while I tried to figure out what to do next.

The other villagers began coming out of their huts, knowing the man had broken the ice, and that I didn't appear to be a threat. Even in my exhaustion, my heart kicked up a couple of beats when someone in the crowd caught my attention. Walking through the doorway of the old man's hut was a beautiful young girl that I immediately recognized. She had sat next to me on the boat trip from Guanay to Mapiri. I remembered offering her a stick of gum and trying to strike up a conversation, but as is often the case in these remote regions, she'd tucked her head in shyness.

The girl came over and stood next to us, staring timidly at the ground. I could see she was smiling, probably flattered that she'd seen the recognition in my eyes. She reached out and took the old man's hand, who I now guessed was her father, and began explaining something to him in their language. I didn't know what was being said, but by the expression on his face, I assumed she was telling him about us meeting on the boat, and hopefully, that I'd treated her with kindness and respect. After surviving the ordeal with the *Sendero Luminoso,* and everything else that I'd been through, I thought what a shame it would be to get my ticket punched by a pissed-off father with a sharp machete.

Apparently, the old man was satisfied with whatever she'd told him, because he began motioning for me to follow them back to their hut.

When we entered their small home, it took a few minutes for my eyes to adjust to the darkness, and then I recognized it as standard fare for villages like this throughout the region. It was poverty in its most basic form. Unlike many of those in the so-called civilized world, these people were satisfied with what they had, instead of constantly worrying about what they didn't have.

The entire place was damp and had the distinct odor of mildew, probably from water that seeped through the thatched roof when it rained. There was a lone flickering candle stuck to the center of a wooden table with two long benches on either side. The walls were white-washed adobe and cracked throughout. The only decoration in the place was a brightly colored calendar proclaiming the political promises of a former presidential candidate. I could see by the date that it was ten years old. Like most of these types of huts, the floor was dirt, swept smooth, and packed down to the consistency of a cement slab. The only thing that seemed to be missing was a crying baby and a handful of small children running around. From what I could see, it appeared that it was just the three of them living there — the girl, her father, and a rotund woman I noticed squatting down in front of a cook fire just outside the back door.

The man pulled back one of the benches, offering me a seat while he barked instructions to his wife out back. The girl busied herself preparing for supper.

I always felt guilty taking anything from families in these remote villages, especially since I knew they barely had enough to sustain themselves. But I also knew that it was their way to share whatever they had. The same man who'd given me the life-saving advice about keeping the small derringer hidden away in my shirt pocket, had also taught me that you should always carry your own cup, plate, and eating utensils. These kind villagers would share whatever food they had, but usually didn't have enough plates to go around. Remembering that sage advice, I reached into my field pack and produced the items. The girl's face lit up with a smile. She quickly took them from me to wash before setting them out on the table.

Because of the language barrier there was no conversation during the meal, but there were lots of smiles and nodding heads. There were also dozens of eyes peeking through windows and around the open doorway, watching the stranger have his meal. To say the least, I felt a little bit like a carnival sideshow.

I knew the custom was to eat around sunset, and then to bed down for the night. I also knew that there were few diversions in life around here beyond the basics of survival. At least tonight, maybe my visit would bring them something to get excited about.

CHAPTER 67

DOMINIQUE LeDeaux unpacked her bags, thinking what a shame it was that she couldn't have done this job when she was here before. Lately, she'd begun to realize that she was tiring of her travels around the world. Some of the excitement was wearing off her unique trade, and she thought more and more about calling it quits.

At the ripe old age of thirty-eight, she already had enough money stashed away to live an extremely comfortable life whether she ever took another assignment or not. She'd also just finished having a beautiful home built overlooking the ocean in a quaint little town on the northern coast of Costa Rica. That was where she found her real pleasure these days.

Dominique hadn't liked the man she'd come to see the last time she was here. She didn't care for his arrogance or his unwelcome advances. That was going to give this job an added bonus — she was going to enjoy it.

Vicente Toscalini had called her only moments after Alan Breckenridge left his home. He'd said that J. Edward had outlived his usefulness, and that he would like her to take care of the matter.

"Immediately," she'd told him. "But for a man of his prominence and position, the fee will be double."

"Done," Toscalini said, and hung up the phone.

In contrast to what most people believe, because of the image portrayed on television and in the movies, the life of a freelance assassin wasn't one of constant work. Common thugs and leg-breakers used to collect past due debts and settle small disputes were one thing. But for a trained killer who would do the job right and never leave a trail back to their client, assignments were few and far between. They were also very profitable. For Dominique LeDeaux, times had been especially good lately, having already had two contracts just this month alone.

Being exceptionally good at what you do always pays off in the long run, and J. Edward Adams III was about to find out just how good she really was.

CHAPTER 68

ALAN Breckenridge stood in room #113 in a run-down motel just off Old Highway 66. It was one of those places that catered mostly to migrant workers, renting bare-bones accommodations by the month. Thomas Williamson had called and said the authorities had been notified of J. Edward's activities, but they needed more details. He said they would meet him here in order to reduce the risk of them being seen together, to help protect his identity.

Breckenridge was glad that he was meeting with state officials, instead of the federal authorities. As much as he wanted to bring J. Edward down, because of his past, there was no way he was ready for a face-to-face with the feds. Thomas Williamson would have to be the one to deal with them, whether he liked it or not.

"Mr. Breckenridge," one of the men began. "We appreciate you coming forward with this information, but there are still a few things we aren't quite clear on."

"What can I do to help?" Breckenridge said.

"Have you brought the original documents with you?"

"Absolutely. I have them right here." He'd also left a complete set of copies in the safe back at his condo. He leaned over to get the paperwork out of his briefcase, and when he straightened back up, he noticed that there was a third man in the room who hadn't been there before.

Apparently, he'd been hiding in the bathroom, and he certainly wasn't someone Breckenridge expected to see.

"Yes, Mr. Breckenridge, there are a few details we aren't quite clear on."

"What in the hell is going on here?" Breckenridge demanded.

"Two of the men who had been seated at a small table stood up, flanking J. Edward Adams III. Both held pistols in their hands.

"What this is, you backstabbing little twit, is your judge and jury," J. Edward said.

Breckenridge knew what was coming next. He didn't even waste the effort of trying to go for the pistol he had holstered under his jacket.

"And sir, we find you guilty of the crime of disloyalty."

One of the men next to J. Edward quickly raised his weapon and shot Breckenridge in the head at point blank range. He fell back on the bed. The .22 caliber slug ricocheted around in his skull, destroying his brain and ending his life. A thin wisp of gray smoke rose from the small red dot in the center of his forehead. The other man leaned forward and shot him three times in the chest, just to make certain that the job was done.

Both killers unscrewed the silencers from their weapons and dropped them into their suit coat pockets. Then, one of them picked up Breckenridge's briefcase. Along with J. Edward, they walked calmly out of the room, leaving Alan Breckenridge dead on the bed.

CHAPTER 69

I DIDN'T have a clue how long I'd been asleep. Exhausted, I'd lost all sense of time. What I did know was that it was pitch black in the hut and that I couldn't get my eyes focused on the face of my watch. As far as I knew I could have been asleep for fifteen minutes, or five hours. I just couldn't tell. I also realized that I wasn't on my bedroll alone. I could feel her warmth curled up at my side and heard her breathing deeply, sound asleep. She must have slipped up next to me during the night.

The family had shared their meager offerings. The old woman had even added meat to what would have been nothing more than weak broth. It was mostly chicken heads and feet, but I'd been honored, knowing they'd been willing to share what little they had with a complete stranger who'd wandered in out of the jungle and into their midst.

After dinner, the old man and I sipped tin mugs of steaming hot coca tea, while the girl and her mother cleared the dishes. I assumed that I'd pitch my bedroll out by the fire, but as it usually is with these gracious people, they wanted me to have the best of what they had to offer.

There was a pile of dried straw stacked in a corner of the hut, and the old man spread it out on the dirt floor, shaping it into the form of a crude mattress. Then, he picked up my bedroll and laid it on top of the makeshift bed. He hung a blanket from a low crossbeam to give me some privacy, and then he and the woman picked up their bedding and went out by the fire. The girl rolled her blanket out on the far side of the room and blew out the candles.

Now, here I was, out in the absolute middle of nowhere, sleeping on a straw bed in an adobe hut, having just finished a supper of chicken-bit soup, with a beautiful young native girl curled up at my side. I laced my arm under her shoulder and pulled her closer. She stirred slightly, rubbing her hand across my bare chest. I kissed her gently on the forehead, and then tried to get some more sleep.

My plan was to leave at daybreak so I could be back in Apolo by midnight. On Friday, I hoped to catch a flight on the C-130 to La Paz, and then a few days later, travel back to the States.

CHAPTER 70

GERALD Parker sat in the front seat of his rented SUV, toying with the little .25 automatic. Eye for an eye. He wanted justice for what had been done to his wife and family, but he was having a tough time building up the courage for what he'd come to do. He could feel the sweat trickling down under his arms, and now that the time was here, he wasn't sure if he could do it or not.

He just sat there, staring at the home of J. Edward Adams III. He was the man Lincoln Mayberry told him owned Frontier Financial Corporation, and who had sent Frank Jacobson to kill him, but instead, had blown up his wife. Images of the days surrounding Janet's death filled his thoughts. The explosion. The burning remains of the car with his sweet, innocent wife trapped inside. Her funeral. The sealed casket because all it contained where what few grisly remains they could find. "What we could scrape off the sidewalk and the side of the house," he'd heard the coroner say. He hadn't even been able to see her face one last time before they lowered her into the ground. And their girls. Their carefree lives shrouded in the grief and sorrow of what they'd seen happen to their mother.

His anger finally boiled over. His courage returned. Gerald Parker kicked open the door and marched toward the front of the mansion with a renewed purpose and determination. He didn't waste time ringing the bell. He wasn't in a courteous mood. He hammered his fist on the door until he got a response. The pistol was gripped tight in his right hand.

The man who opened the door wasn't at all what he expected. Then, reality sank in. *Of course, a man like this Adams guy wouldn't answer his own door,* he thought.

His plan had been to pound on the door until J. Edward opened it, and then blow the bastard away. But now what?

"I…I…I want to see Mr. Adams." Parker's words tumbled out in a nervous stutter. He gripped the pistol even tighter, holding it behind his leg.

"Mr. Adams is entertaining guests and cannot be disturbed," the butler said, dignified and calm, just as he had been trained to do. He began to push the door closed.

Parker jammed his foot in the doorway. "I don't give a damn what he's doing! I want to see him, right now!" he demanded.

A voice came from behind the butler and a man appeared around the corner of the hallway.

That's got to be him, Parker thought.

As the butler turned to see who was coming up behind him, Gerald Parker jerked up the pistol and fired off three quick shots. His inexperience was immediately evident. The first two rounds went wild, doing nothing more than punching holes into the wall. By nothing but pure luck, the third shot struck the man in his right upper thigh.

Three shots were all he'd get off.

The butler quickly stepped back and drew a .45 automatic from under his jacket. He fired one quick-kill round into the center of Parker's chest. His body crumpled onto the front porch.

The butler had been a British SAS offer before retiring from service to his country and coming to work for J. Edward. And like most of J. Edward's employees, he thoroughly enjoyed playing his skills. He holstered the weapon, and then calmly called 911 on his cellphone.

Many of the female guests had heard the gunplay and were screaming. Other guests ran to the front of the house to try and see what was going on. J. Edward was first on the scene.

The butler kicked the pistol away from Parker's hand. He leaned down and touched two fingers to his neck, feeling for a pulse. He was confident that there wouldn't be one, but he knew appearances were important at a time like this.

"I don't know what happened, sir," he said to J. Edward. "He just started shooting and I did what had to be done to protect Mr. Clifford." He tipped his chin toward the man who'd been shot in the leg, writhing in pain on the floor behind them. He was one of the guests who had been expecting some contracts to be delivered that needed J. Edward's signature. That was why he'd gone to the front of the house when he'd heard the banging on the door.

"It's alright, Jensen, you had no other choice," J. Edward said, acting as if he were trying to console the man. It was all a big show. He knew that as soon as his guests were gone, he and Jenson would share a brandy and he would listen to him brag about how he'd "blown the bastard away".

J. Edward wouldn't find out from the police until later that the man lying dead on his front porch was Gerald Parker. Then, he would feel a moment of even greater satisfaction, knowing that one more problem had been dealt with.

CHAPTER 71

I GOT back home late last night. The night I spent in Pata with the native girl curled up at my side was the last decent sleep I'd had. I wasn't able to catch a flight on the C-130 out of Apolo because of foul weather, and the overland trip to La Paz had taken three grueling days. I'd gotten one night of fitful sleep at the Hotel Copacabana, and then endured the long flight back to the States.

Most people don't understand the serious shock your body takes coming back from an extended period of time having to survive the rigors of life in the jungle. For me, it's harder to adjust to being back in civilization than it is acclimating to going into the bush. The jungle seems more like home now.

After arriving at my apartment, I'd pitched my unpacked bags on the floor, taken a long, soaking hot shower, and planned to sleep through most of the next day.

No such luck.

Eight o'clock in the morning and someone was banging on my door. As far as I knew, nobody even knew I was back. Still in jungle mode, I slipped the 9mm off the nightstand and went to see who it was. I stood adjacent to the door with my back pressed against the wall. Old habits die hard.

"Yeah, who is it?"

"Delivery. I have a package for Mr. Damien Chance. It has to be signed for."

I was standing there in nothing but a pair of blue briefs. That left nowhere to hide the pistol. What the hell. I opened the door, holding the 9mm in plain sight.

The deliveryman gasped and stepped back.

"Whatcha' got? I asked, acting like answering the door semi-naked with a pistol in my hand was the normal thing to do.

"Sign on line twenty-six, please," he said, nervously holding out his clipboard.

I reached out with my left hand and scribbled my signature.

"There you go," I said.

"And there you go," he said, handing me the package.

"Sorry," I said, slapping my hand against my leg. "No pockets, no tip."

"Not a problem, sir." He was just glad to be getting out of there in one piece. He'd have a hell of a story to tell when he got back to his office.

I watched him stumble down the stairs and out into the parking lot, sprinting to his truck.

I kicked the door closed and walked over to sit at the kitchen table, startling when the cold vinyl hit the back of my bare legs. I laid the pistol down and looked at the return label on the package. *The Law Offices of Everett Ferguson, San Francisco, California.* No street address. No telephone number. Never heard of him.

I ripped it open and saw several banded stacks of hundred-dollar bills, and immediately knew who it was really from. I didn't even have to count the money. There would be a hundred grand, just like Don Taylor said I'd receive after the job was done.

As much as I could use the cash, I hadn't even thought about it with all that had been going on. Now that I had it, I wasn't sure what the hell to do with it.

I peeled off enough to settle some bills and to cover expenses for a few weeks. Later, I'd go to the bank and rent a safety deposit box and squirrel the rest of it away for a rainy day.

I wondered if the money would make me feel like all that I'd done, and all that I'd been through, was worth it.

I went back to bed. I was still about eighteen hours away from having all the sleep my body was telling me I needed.

CHAPTER 72

LISA Dalton sat on the floor of the bedroom she and Alan had shared. She was no longer upset about how he'd deceived her, knowing that it wouldn't do any good. He was gone. "Shot once in the head and three times in the chest," the detective had told her.

Reliving bad memories would do nothing more than make the situation worse, so she decided to reminisce about the good times they'd had. She flipped through the pages of a photo album from one of their vacations. They'd gone to Maui for ten glorious days, relishing each and every second like there would never be another time like the one they had right then and there. She reached up and touched the pearl that hung from a delicate gold chain around her neck. Alan had bought it for her when they were in Hawaii. Tears filled her eyes. She closed the album. It was just too much to deal with.

She got up and went over to a framed Monet print hanging on the bedroom wall. Swinging it back on its hinges exposed the safe concealed behind it. Alan had given her the combination when he had it installed. She'd never had any use for it before, but now she thought maybe there was something in there that would reveal more truth about the man she *thought* she knew. The man who'd broken her heart. The man who'd been shot once in the head and three times in the chest. The man she would always love.

CHAPTER 73

THE smoke was as thick as ever and the music played loud enough to vibrate in my bones. It felt good to be back. Mike sidled up next to me, leaning over and yelling in my ear. "When are you going to be ready to come back to work? I need you around here," he said.

I was leaned up against one of the bars at the Stone Horse Club, losing myself in the noise, the smoke, and the music. It was just like it was that first night I'd met Don Taylor. But tonight, I wasn't working. I was just having a cold beer and visiting with a few friends, surveying my old stomping grounds.

"I don't know," I said. "I'll let you know in a week or two."

"No problem-o," Mike said. "Whenever you're ready, you've always got a spot around here." He flowed back into the crowd, leaving me alone with my thoughts and my beer.

"I guess old habits die hard," said the man who'd moved up next to me.

I glanced over and almost dropped my cup when I saw who it was.

"I swear, I'm starting to think you slipped a tracking device up my ass," I laughed.

Don Taylor smiled and raised his beer. I raised mine and we tapped cups.

"Before you even ask, I don't want anything," he said. "I just came by to see how you're doing."

Taylor was a master at what he did, and when he looked into Chance's eyes, he could see how this last job had affected him. He could tell that he was worn down a bit, but he could also see that special fire that was still burning inside him. Once again, he was convinced that his initial instincts about him had been right on target.

"That's good," I said. "Because right now, I'm just plain old worn out." I continued surveying the action on the floor.

"That's too bad. I was going to pay a visit to the man who sent those shooters after you down in La Paz," Taylor said, dropping the little bombshell right into Chance's lap.

"What?"

"Yep, he's right here in Oklahoma City. And believe it or not, he's also the sick bastard that was behind sending Gerald Parker down to your camp."

I turned and looked him square in the eye.

"Chance, he was partners with Ramiro Dueñas, and then with Colonel Zoto."

"So, what you're telling me is, he was involved in the raid on our camp? For killing Cristina and my men?" I felt sick to my stomach.

"I'm afraid so. He's some big-shot business tycoon and the one those drugs from Colonel Zoto were coming to."

I just stared at him.

"What to take a ride?" he asked.

"Let's rock-and-roll," I said.

CHAPTER 74

DOMINIQUE LeDeaux stepped out of the shower, slipping into the luxurious hotel bathrobe. She cinched the belt tight around her narrow waist and opened the door, letting the porter roll in the room service cart.

It was nine-thirty and she planned on enjoying a late supper in her room, watching the news, and then getting dressed to pay a late-night visit to J. Edward Adams III. She called him earlier and said that she had reconsidered his offer of employment and wondered if they might meet to discuss the opportunity. "Of course," he said, telling her that the only place he would be able to meet her would be at his home. She lied and told him she would be flying in from Chicago, and that she could be there by eleven-thirty if that wasn't too late. "Not at all, my dear. That will be perfect," he said.

Dominique knew that J. Edward was planning on offering her much more than just a job. She could hear the sick, giddy excitement in his voice. It made her skin crawl to even think about what he had in mind.

CHAPTER 75

O N the drive over form the Stone Horse, Taylor brought me up to speed on all that had happened while I was out of contact down in the Amazon. He told me about J. Edward's connection to Gerald Parker, and about how his wife had been blown up, and about Parker himself being killed. Then, he told me about Frank Jacobson and Alan Breckenridge, and how both of them had been murdered. When he told me about Agent Donaldson, it brought a smile to my face.

"I knew I popped the right asshole that first night," I said.

"That's exactly what I told his partner," Taylor laughed.

I told him about everything that had taken place down in Bolivia and Peru. I told him about Colonel Zoto and my dealings with the *Sendero Luminoso*, and just as I expected, he loved it all.

Taylor pulled the car up against the curb across from J. Edward's mansion.

"I thought we'd go in together and ask him a few questions," Taylor said. "Still interested, or would you rather wait in the car?" He grinned.

"Screw waiting in the car," I said. "Let's go!"

CHAPTER 76

J. EDWARD was visibly nervous. It was a condition he wasn't used to, and one he certainly wasn't enjoying at the moment. He'd given Jensen, his butler/bodyguard, the night off in anticipation of his meeting with Dominique LeDeaux. He was confident that she would be staying the night.

When the bell rang, he pulled open both heavy French doors in a dramatic fashion. Standing there was an exceptionally beautiful woman, but she certainly wasn't what he expected. There were no greetings or pleasantries, just the barrel of a very threatening nickel-plated revolver aimed right at his chest. He backed into the entryway and she followed, never taking the weapon from her target.

"Sit down!" she ordered, once they were in the living room. J. Edward complied. It's tough to argue when you're on the receiving end of a loaded gun.

"What do you want?" he asked.

"I want you to shut up!" she said.

He looked up at the beautiful woman.

Deadly silence.

Then, there was the violent crack of a shot. A small crimson dot punctuated J. Edward's chest. Blood seeped out slowly and a dark red stain the size of a dinner plate formed on the front of his crisp white shirt. His mouth was wide open, and he struggled for breath.

She stepped forward and shot him twice more.

And just like that, it was over. J. Edward's plans for greatness were finished. Right there in his home, a beautiful woman had delivered his just reward. She finished what had to be done. She dropped the pistol into her purse and walked out the front door.

CHAPTER 77

AS Taylor and I walked up to the edge of J. Edward's manicured lawn, we saw a woman double-timing it down the driveway. She didn't even acknowledge our presence. She jumped into her car, and tires squealing, sped off into the night.

"That's odd," Taylor said, looking toward the front of the mansion. Both ornate doors were pulled wide open and bright light from inside the house poured out across the lawn.

We approached cautiously, drawn pistols at the ready. As we got closer, we could both smell the distinct odor of gunpowder in the air.

I was the first to make the discovery.

"Taylor, you better come take a look at this."

Both of us stood there, staring down at the body.

"Is that our man?" I asked.

"Yep," Taylor said, nodding.

"Do you think that woman is the one that killed him?"

"Who cares," Taylor said. "Someone's done the job for us. Let's just get the hell out of here before we have to explain ourselves to the cops."

CHAPTER 78

OMINIQUE LeDeaux pulled her car slowly past the front of J.
Edward's mansion. There was a crowd of curious neighbors milling
around on the lawn. The front doors were standing wide open and
two attendants with CORONER stenciled across the back of their blue
jumpsuits wheeled out a gurney with a large black body bag riding on
top. There were at least five police cruisers parked at various angles
in the street with their red and blue lights flashing. Police radio chat-
ter filled the night air. She continued to drive slowly past the crowd
until she noticed one of the neighbors walking down the street, away
from the house. She pulled up next to the woman and powered down
her window.

"Excuse me, ma'am, but what's all the commotion about?"

"Oh honey, someone has killed Mr. Adams," she said.

"Are you sure?" Dominique asked.

"Oh, yes. They shot him dead, right there in his living room,"
she lamented.

Dominique tapped the switch and her window hissed back up.
She drove slowly out of J. Edward's neighborhood.

CHAPTER 79

LISA Dalton stood at the wall safe in her condo. She swung open the heavy steel door and laid the pistol back where she'd found it. It had been on top of the copies of the paperwork that Alan had compiled on his business dealings with J. Edward Adams III. Seeing all that documentation, Lisa realized that he had been trying to bring the man down. Unfortunately, it also showed all his involvement in the organization as well. At least now she knew the real reason he was dead, and the reason that her heart was broken.

When Lisa was a young girl, her father had taught her how to handle a gun. "Hopefully, you'll never need to know how to use one," he'd said. "But I would rather you know how and never need it, than to need it and not know how.

When she'd picked up that pistol, it felt comfortable in her hands.

Today, she needed to know how.

She'd taken that weapon and finished what needed to be done and settled the score with J. Edward Adams III.

CHAPTER 80

DON Taylor and I sat at a corner table at the back of the diner. I ordered coffee, black, no cream, no sugar. I tipped my chair back, balancing it on two legs, leaning against the wall. Both of our minds were stretched at the seams with all that had happened.

"The evil men will do for money and power never ceases to amaze me," Taylor said, thinking about the cast of characters he and Chance had dealt with.

I didn't say anything. My mind was churning with all that had happened since this nightmare began. I thought about the death, the misery, and the retribution. I was deep into considering what my own hand had to do with it all, and where I'd go from here.

"Chance, when we first met, I told you that I would try and help you to stop those demons eating away at your conscience and give you the opportunity to settle the score for that attack on your camp, and for what they did to Cristina. I don't know about the demons, but you damn sure settled the score, and then some," he said.

I knew I'd waded off into the stinking muck and mire of vengeance, and that I'd gone in on my own accord. It was my decision to do the things that I'd done, and I believed that I'd done what was right. I could live with that.

"Everyone isn't cut out for this kind of work. They don't have the instincts to survive or the mental steel to live with themselves afterwards," Taylor said. He reached down and pulled something out of his pocket, holding it in his palm, and rubbing it with the tip of his thumb. "It isn't an easy life, but I truly believe you've got what it takes. More importantly, I think you believe it, too."

I dropped my chair back down so all four legs were square on the tile floor. Then, I took one last sip of coffee and stood up.

Taylor pitched the thing he'd pulled out of his pocket onto the table. It made a solid thud, and then wobbled around for a few seconds before coming to a rest. I looked down and saw that it was a silver and black medallion. There was an ominous-looking skull in the center, hovering over an image of the world that was bordered by palm trees. It was highlighted with the words, *Outlaw Traveler*. I reached down and picked it up, clutching it tight in my fist, nodding that I understood the significance. Then, I reached out and gripped Taylor's hand, sealing our bond for the work we both believed needed to be done.

"Call me when you need me," I said. Then, I turned and walked out into the night, committing myself to the life of an *Outlaw Traveler*.

ABOUT THE AUTHOR

DENNIS Hambright has spent over twenty-five years working as a private investigator and security consultant, handling assignments throughout the United States, Central America, South America, and Southeast Asia. Before that, he worked as a banker, salesman, repo man, bouncer, bodyguard, and radio personality. He spent four years living in Bolivia, searching for gold and lost treasure in the jungles of the Amazon basin, and five years living in Costa Rica.

For more information, you can visit the author's website:

DennisHambright.com